The Private Investigator

San Francisco

Ken Ewell

THE PRIVATE INVESTIGATOR
SAN FRANCISCO

iUniverse books may be ordered through booksellers or by contacting:

iUniverse LLC
1663 Liberty Drive
Bloomington, IN 47403
www.iuniverse.com
1-800-Authors (1-800-288-4677)

ISBN: 978-1-4917-4363-8 (sc)
ISBN: 978-1-4917-4362-1 (e)

Library of Congress Control Number: 2014914250

Printed in the United States of America.

iUniverse rev. date: 08/08/2014

*Dedicated to the Private Investigator,
who's often the only arbiter of justice
in the back alleys of the naked city.*

Contents

San Francisco

A Dry Martini in Specs'

Private investigator Sam Marlowe was sitting at his usual table in Specs' Twelve Adler Museum Cafe at 12 William Saroyan Place in North Beach. From that stakeout he could look up at the old photo of Humphrey Bogart above the table while enjoying his usual libation, a very dry gin martini with two olives. He was comfortable in Specs', and not just for the presence of his mentor Bogey. He liked that bar for it was home to an assortment of bric-a-brac that paid homage to the guys and dolls that once called San Francisco home. That is, before the city turned itself into a T-shirt town, one now referred to by the old-timers as "Chardonnay by the Bay" or "The 21st Arrondissement of Paris." It also reminded him of the days when bars were home to men who drank like men, and to women who also drank like men.

Sam drank that night to celebrate the solving of his most recent investigation, one he'd named "The Case of the Gyrating Gender." He liked naming his cases; it entertained him and it made them seem important. Of course they weren't terribly important, for the PI business had changed a great deal since the glory days of the "hard-boiled" detective, thanks mainly to the legalization of no-fault divorce. As is now common knowledge, by the Seventies everyone and his son were fooling around on their wives, and vice versa, so the courts simply threw up their hands in desperation. At that time, many of the PIs retired from the business. And those that remained took on different and sometimes strange cases, especially in San Francisco.

Sam's latest case was the sort he occasionally worked on in the city, that being for clients who were unsure about their gender identity. Unbeknownst to those who don't live in San Francisco, many individuals from all over America travel west to determine their sexual identity, usually beginning that search in a rather well-known neighborhood off Market Street. And when that search uncovered no clues and produced even more gender confusion, they came to him for help. Sam never truly understood this sort of case for his view of the world remained forever the same as his two dads: One's sex was what was indicated on one's birth certificate... period.

"The Case of the Gyrating Gender" involved a man who underwent a sex change, after which, she became uncertain about her decision. So she hired Sam to help her determine her true gender identity, which turned out to actually be a man. The result was another sex change, with both operations paid for by the city. Fortunately, he compensated Sam with a tidy sum to sort out the problem. But despite his pleasant pecuniary gain, Sam still shook his head at this type of case while thinking to himself: "Only in San Francisco." Undoubtedly, his two dads were probably rolling over in their graves laughing about what had happened to the PI trade. And just like his dads, at the end of each investigation he prepared a report for his client that explained the details of the completed case.

Just then, Specs' bartender caught Sam's attention and asked if he needed another one. Sam nodded yes, and within a few moments there was a second martini sitting on the bar. Returning to the table with his drink, Sam heard some commotion near the piano at the back of the saloon. A local piano player, Cricket, and a female singer, Slim, were just beginning a session with the classic song, *Am I Blue*. And as her name implied, she was quite slender, except where it counted most.

That night, the tune struck Sam as appropriate for the melancholic mood that he was always in at the end of any case. At times like this Sam reflected on his life, one that was somewhat uncommon, though not necessarily in San Francisco. Although the actual facts of his story were never told directly to him, he pieced the account together over the years. This was generally done when his two private investigator dads, Samuel Spade and Philip Marlowe, had had a few too many drinks, which was most of the time. Partners after the war, Sam and Phil had been working a case together in San Francisco and Los Angeles. After finishing it up, they took Effie Perine, Sam's secretary, out for dinner and drinks.

Apparently they all had a snoot-full of gin and eventually staggered back to Sam's apartment, where Effie rewarded both detectives for a case well-solved. Needless to say, young Sam's mom never knew who his dad really was, and the science wasn't there in those days to make a case one way or the other. Anyway, that's how he ended up with the name Sam Marlowe, as well as how he ended up in the PI business. Of course, his name could just as well have been Phil Spade, but that's not how it turned out.

Sam grew up thinking of each man as his dad, spending the school-year in San Francisco with his mom and Sam senior, and learning the ins and outs of the PI business after school and on weekends. During the summer his mom and SF dad sent him south to spend time in Los Angeles with his other dad, Phil, who taught him the ins and outs of the PI trade as well. Also during the summer, and when not working on a case with the old man, he'd spend time at the beach reading stories of other cases his two dads worked on. And what great investigations they were, with Dashiell Hammett chronicling one of Sam senior's cases in the *The Maltese Falcon*, and Raymond Chandler doing the same in four of Phil's cases: *The Big Sleep*, *Farewell My Lovely*, *The High Window*, and *The Lady in the Lake*. Needless to say, though trained by the best in the business, Sam was no "hard-boiled" detective like his two dads. No, he was barely "soft-boiled." But it passed for a life anyway, at least in these less than manly times and this less than manful city.

The Siren in the Sea

Sam was about ready to head next door to Tosca Cafe at 242 Columbus Avenue for a bite to eat when he heard the buzzer on his phone, which always called to him with the *Peter Gunn Theme*. He heard a familiar women's voice on the other end. "Sam, I need your help. Please come down to The Club immediately."

Sam hesitated for a moment, for he'd told himself a year back to never have anything to do with this dazzling dame again. But "once a chump, always a chump," so he reluctantly replied, "OK, Cosette, I'll be there as quickly as I can." Draining what was left of his martini, he made his way out of Specs'. Little did he know as he hit the street and hailed a cab, this was the beginning of "The Case of the Siren in the Sea."

As the cab headed north on Columbus Avenue, Sam thought back to when he first met Cosette a year and a half back:

I was working a private party in the basement The Club that night when I first saw Cosette performing as "The Siren in the Sea." I marveled at how realistic she appeared as she seemingly swam in the sea, waving her arms as if an ancient Siren. Of course in reality it was an illusion, with her foot-long image projected onto the back of the aquarium. But what really caught my attention that night was Cosette, who performed without a stitch of clothing, nothing to hide, not even her womanly virtue.

Cosette had dark honey blond hair, a shade that reminded me of ambrosia, the golden nectar beloved by the ancient gods. Her eyes were a shade of brown as dark as a moonless night. Her face was almost goddess-like as she beamed an iridescent smile that lit up the room. And Cosette had such a voluptuous figure that the sight of it would cause a priest to forget even his favorite altar boy.

Once the performance was over, Cosette changed and went upstairs to the bar. With the private gathering ended and the group filing out of the club, a drunk from the party approached her. She told him to leave her alone, but he continued to persist. I saw the commotion and walked over to help her. I grabbed the drunk, marched him to the door, and then tossed him out of the club and onto the street.

I returned to the bar to check on Cosette, who was still irritated about the incident. She told me to sit and have a drink with her. I ordered a martini for myself and she ordered her usual drink, a whiskey on the rocks. We made small-talk for some time until I asked her why she let unfamiliar men see her completely naked in "The Siren in the Sea" illusion. Cosette's answer intrigued me, for she responded, "Aren't all women seen in an aquarium by men? Don't men always see what they want to see?"

With their drinks finished, Cosette asked me if I would escort her back to her apartment, just in case the drunk was still outside. I agreed, and we walked without incident to her place. She then asked me to come upstairs for a nightcap, which brought about the start of a six-month affair that ended poorly for me.

As the cab continued along Columbus, Sam noticed that Washington Square was crowded with cops, paramedics and loads of vehicles. After a few more blocks he got out at The Club and went in through the doors. He hadn't been there in a year, but it was still the same old place. Sam found Cosette at the bar, shaken up and very tense. She said to him, "Sam, there's been a shooting in Washington Square. I was on the phone with a long-time friend who told me that she was in the Square and that it looked like they were going to take the two girls. I then heard a shot and the line went dead. Please, Sam, go find out what's being done about my friend and the girls."

Sam replied, "I'll see what I can find out."

"Thanks, Sam," Cosette responded, "I knew I could count on you."

Sam walked a few blocks up Columbus to Washington Square, where most of the cops were gathered around the Benjamin Franklin statue in the middle of the park. He noticed his friend, Tom, a police Detective-sergeant, who asked, "What are you doing here, Sam? This isn't your sort of business."

"Just helping out a friend," Sam answered. "What's going on here?"

"As near as I can figure," Tom explained, "it appears that one of the strippers from the joints over on Broadway was shot and killed about a half hour ago. However, something seems a little fishy. Earlier I spotted a homeless guy on one of the park benches. For a sawbuck he told me that the dead woman was with two young girls a few minutes before the shooting. He said that then a van ran onto the asphalt walkway that crosses the Square and a man got out. According to the bum, he shot the woman near the Franklin statue, pushed the girls into his car and then drove off. The problem is, Sam, that guy has now disappeared, probably in a bar somewhere."

Just then, the Lieutenant came over to Sam and Tom. Looking at Sam, he angrily said, "You have no business here, Marlowe. This has nothing to do with you, so clear out and stay away from police affairs."

Sam had had run-ins with this dick before and didn't like the guy, a bad sort, even for a cop. But this time his attitude was completely out of line and Sam was suspicious of his motives. So he asked the Lieutenant, "Tom said there may have been a couple of young girls in the park when the shooting occurred. What can you tell me about that?"

The Lieutenant first looked at Tom, giving him a bad look, and then answered Sam, "We don't know anything about two girls and this is strictly a case of homicide, some Broadway stripper. So I don't want to hear about you sticking your nose into this case. It's strictly department business."

He walked away and Sam said to Tom, "Keep that guy away from me."

"Sam, I'd do as he says," Tom warned. "I'm not sure what's going on here, but it clearly goes further than department business. How about if I call you in the morning once I find out more?"

"Thanks, that's fine, Tom," Sam responded. "But still, keep that guy away from me. As you know, nobody tells Sam Marlowe what to do." Sam then walked back down Columbus to The Club and Cosette.

A Candid Conversation in Vesuvio

As soon as Sam got back to Cosette, she said to him, "Why don't we get out of this place. How about if we head over to Vesuvio for a drink so I can tell you what's going on."

Cosette and Sam left The Club and caught a cab back down the avenue to Vesuvio at 255 Columbus Avenue and Jack Kerouac Alley, across from Specs'. They walked in the door and managed to find Cosette's preferred first-floor table empty. She always liked sitting in the wicker chair that faced away from Broadway, though she'd never told him why in the six months they were together. When the waitress arrived, she ordered her usual whiskey, and he his martini.

While Cosette sipped at her drink and calmed herself, Sam looked over this other bar he hadn't been in for a year. The two floors of Vesuvio were a shrine to Jack Kerouac, the Beat Generation writer who penned the classic *On the Road*. However, it wasn't Jack that coined the name "Beatnik," a combination of Beat and Sputnik, but the famed San Francisco journalist Herb Caen in his *San Francisco Chronicle* column of April 2, 1958: "*Look* magazine, preparing a picture spread on SF's Beat Generation (oh, no, not again!), hosted a party in a North Beach house for 50 Beatniks, and by the time word got around the sour grapevine, over 250 bearded cats and kits were on hand, slopping up Mike Cowles' free booze. They're only Beat, y'know, when it comes to work."

The bar was somewhat quiet that night, which allowed Sam to listen in to Jack, a regular at his usual table, relay his *On the Road* thoughts to an attentive kitten: "... leaving confusion and nonsense behind and performing our one noble function of the time, move.... all the golden land's ahead of you and all kinds of unforeseen events wait lurking to surprise you and make you glad you're alive to see.... the sordid hipsters of America, a new beat generation that [I] was slowly joining.... What was I doing? Where was I going? I'd soon find out... the road is life.... What's your road, man?... holyboy road, madman road, rainbow road, guppy road, or any road. It's an anywhere road for anybody anyhow."

While delivering his up-Beat message, Vesuvio was filled with the melody that always reminded a traveler to return to the road: Nat King Cole's original version of *Route 66*. Once the road memories ended, Sam looked at Cosette and asked, "How are you connected with this killing in Washington Square?"

"Sam," Cosette began, "the story I'm going to tell you now is one I couldn't tell you a year ago. As you well know, I'm rather top heavy, with my breasts developing at a very young age. And beginning in my early teens, they drew so much attention from boys that I began to identify myself almost solely by them. This is one of the sad things about a girl's adolescence. If she has a large pair, that's how she's characterized by her peers. And if she has a small set, that's how she's portrayed as well. And though you're a man, I'm sure you can imagine what this does to a young women's sense of self-esteem.

"After leaving high school and attending community college for awhile, I decided that if that's how the world was going to see me, then I might as well make a living out of them. So in my twenties I became an exotic dancer down in Southern California, working in clubs that didn't require me to bare anything but my breasts. Then one day in late 1999, a long-time friend from school called and convinced me to move to San Francisco. Since I needed a change of scenery anyway, I tossed what little I had in my car and drove north.

"Unfortunately, my car broke down on the way and it took all the money I had to fix it. Finally in the city, I took the only job that could make me some quick cash. A Broadway club owner was more than willing to hire a larger gal such as myself, so I ended up back on stage as an exotic dancer. However, whereas down south I never had to take everything off, in oh-so-liberal San Francisco it was required that I strip naked. The first time on stage, I was mortified to be seen exposing everything to a crowd of men. And when one of them yelled, 'What can I get for twenty bucks?' I almost fell to pieces.

"Returning to my lonely room that first night, I was so despondent that I came very close to ending my life. I could see no direction in which to turn, no way to get myself out of that fix. Fortunately, I wasn't hooked on drugs or booze like so many of the gals. That's what keeps many of them trapped in the clubs, with exotic dancing, lap dancing, even prostitution the only way to satisfy their habits. But with the help of some of my friends, I got out of the clubs and vowed never to return. And Sam, I think you've often wondered why I always like to sit in this wicker chair. Well, it faces away from Broadway, allowing me to feel protected from the exploitation I experienced in that earlier life.

"I decided that though I desperately needed to get out of exotic dancing, I still enjoyed dancing as a performance art. So I chose a new stage name, Cosette, which I used when performing in burlesque and other dance shows. I selected the name 'Cosette' because it reminded me of the exploited girl in Victor Hugo's *Les Misérables*. And at that time I also vowed to myself that if I was ever in a position to do so, I'd help out other exploited young women. Of course, all that happened over ten years ago.

"As you already know, since then I've made a living as a fitness and Pilates instructor, along with taking part in dance performances and as 'The Siren in the Sea'. However, two years back a friend of mine who still worked as a Broadway performer told me about some of the really young girls that were now working in the clubs. She told me that early on, management was getting them hooked on drugs. And once hooked, using them to make money in the private rooms reserved for well-connected patrons.

"I was so angered by this that I told my friend that if she was ever able to secret any of those exploited young girls out of the clubs, that she should bring them to me. I'd protect them in my apartment through the night and then drive them to my mom's place up in the wine country early the next morning. My mom could then nurse them back to health, counsel them, and hopefully return them to their families. This was precisely what was to happen tonight, except that my friend, who'd contacted me a few days ago, was killed bringing two young underage twins to me."

Visibly concerned, Cosette stopped there, giving Sam a chance to say, "Though what you're doing is highly commendable, do you have any idea how dangerous this is for anyone involved, especially yourself? The guys that manage the clubs on Broadway are no Boy Scouts, and they'll stop at nothing to keep the money rolling in."

Sam then flagged down the waitress and ordered another round. With the fresh drinks on the way, he continued, "You know I was very surprised when you abruptly broke things off with me a year ago. I thought our relationship was going well and that you enjoyed spending time with me. What happened, Cosette?"

"Well, Sam," she responded, "I'll be completely open and honest with you. Do you know not once did you ever spend the night after having sex with me? It was as if you were only comfortable going to bed with 'The Siren in the Sea', but frightened to ever wake up with Cosette. You must know that 'The Siren in the Sea' is only an act, it's not real, and it's just an illusion. There was also the problem of your work as a private investigator. The violence you contended with on a regular basis frightened me, along with the fact that you always carried a gun. I knew you needed it for your work, but the sight of it petrified me. I suppose those are the two main reasons why I broke things off with you."

"You know I'm not by nature a violent man," Sam defended himself. "Why, I don't even load my gun, except on very special occasions. I really carry it so that from time to time I can pistol-whip a man, and then only when he's fully deserving of it. Anyway, you've given me a lot of things to think about tonight, but it's getting too late now."

Sam and Cosette finished their drinks over some small talk, and then made their way out of Vesuvio. She wanted to walk, so he escorted her back along Columbus to her apartment. As they passed Washington Square, all was quiet and only a few homeless stood watch over the park. Before entering her place, Cosette said to him, "Thanks for everything tonight, Sam. I knew I could count on you."

Sam then told her, "I'll call you in the morning once I know more about the two girls." He then went out to Columbus and hailed a cab that took him to his place on Post Street. Once in bed, he thought: "I don't know anything about women." And for the next hour or so he thought about nothing but Cosette while listening to Chet Baker's rendition of *Old Devil Moon*.

Union Square and Financial District

A Private Investigator in San Francisco

The next morning Sam woke up at the usual time in his apartment at 891 Post Street #401, which overlooked the intersection of Post and Hyde Street. He lay in the Murphy bed only briefly before rising and going to the kitchen at the other end of his studio. Once there, he put on a pot of super-strong coffee, not that distasteful swill preferred by the annoying denizens that had taken over San Francisco these days, the ones known as Generation L, for Latte. While the coffee brewed, he went to the bathroom, sat on the throne, and then splashed a little cold water on his face, just to get the previous night's martinis out of his eyes.

Sam returned to the kitchen, poured himself a cuppa java, no milk, and returned to his bed with the straight undiluted stuff that mornings were made for in this coffee-obsessed town. Eventually noticing the clock, Sam got up and pushed his bed back against the wall. He then returned to the kitchen and poured himself another cuppa joe before heading into the bathroom for a shit, a shower, and a shave.

After drying off, Sam went into the closet that sat behind the wall bed. The entire back of it was home to half a dozen identical black suits, a dozen identical white shirts, a handful of identical black ties, and one never-worn red tie given to him by Cosette when they were seeing each other. On the floor there were several identical black belts, loads of identical black socks, and a few pairs of identical black shoes. Sam was a creature of habit and wore the same specially-made attire every day, the same in fact that Sam senior had worn every day of his life.

Surprisingly, the only difference between the dad and the son was the choice of hat. The style Sam senior had worn always made Sam look like a member of the Village People. Fortunately, many years before he'd noticed Frank Sinatra wearing a black fedora on an album cover, and he realized that anyone wearing that particular hat could never be mistaken for someone living in The Castro. And once he realized how good he looked in it, he immediately ordered several identical ones from a hat shop in The Fillmore.

Now dressed, Sam returned to the kitchen and poured himself a third cup of super-strong coffee from the soon-to-be empty pot. Needless to say, his mind was almost ready to confront the day as he sat down on the living room couch that lay against the wall and under the window overlooking Post. He enjoyed this time of the morning, for it gave him the opportunity to think back on when his dad lived here many years before. It was in this apartment that Sam senior slept with Brigid O'Shaughnessy and then made breakfast for her the next morning. It was also here that the two of them walked in on Casper Gutman, Joel Cairo and Wilmer Cook, who were all demanding the return of the Maltese falcon. And after some negotiations, Effie Perine brought the black bird to the apartment, though it turned out to be a fake.

After that, Brigid admitted to using Floyd Thursby and Captain Jacobi to get the black bird for herself. So having a pair of unexplained stiffs on their hands, Sam concocted a scheme whereby the young punk Cook would be fingered for killing both Thursby and Jacobi. Once the other three left, Sam senior figured out that Brigid killed his partner Miles Archer, a fact that he knew must be reconciled with the cops.

In the next moment, in walked Lieutenant Dundy, Detective-sergeant Tom Polhaus and two other detectives. They reported that Cook killed Gutman, and that they'd arrested Cook and Cairo. When they left, the cops also took in Brigid for the murder of Miles Archer, which cleared Sam senior's name of any wrongdoing.

Finally ready to confront the day with a clear head, Sam put on his shoulder holster, fitted his gun into it, and placed his coat on. He then walked down the L-shaped corridor and left the apartment. After making his way down the stairs to street level, he walked out the front door that faced Post. Once on the street, Sam paused for only a moment to read the plaque on the building.

> ### *Home of Dashiell Hammett and Sam Spade*
>
> Dashiell Hammett (1896-1961) lived in this building from 1926 to 1929 when he wrote his first three novels *Red Harvest* (1929), *The Dain Curse* (1929), and *The Maltese Falcon* (1930). Sam Spade's apartment in *The Maltese Falcon* is modeled on Hammett's, which was on the northwest corner of the fourth floor.

Of course the plaque wasn't completely accurate, what plaques ever are? For in fact, Sam's dad had actually taken the struggling writer in as a supposedly temporary roommate, but then couldn't get rid of him for three years. And the promises of royalties from *The Maltese Falcon*, they were as fake as the black bird itself. No matter, PIs are used to seeing stiffs and getting stiffed, for that's part of the profession.

Sam walked east on Post to Leavenworth Street, then north on Leavenworth to Sutter Street. On the southwest corner of the intersection was his usual breakfast place, the same one he'd eaten in for decades. The Golden Coffee Shop at 901 Sutter Street is old school, with a horseshoe counter that allows patrons to constantly spy on and show disdain for one another. With his first cup of high-octane coffee in front of him, Sam ordered his usual, the Number 2: two eggs over easy, hash browns dripping in grease, and sourdough toast with globs of real butter, or what passed for butter in these pitiful times.

When his breakfast arrived in front of him, Sam looked at the plate and thought: "Eggs are the only easy things in a PI's daily routine." As an everyday ritual taught to him by his dad, he rolled his eggs on top of the hash browns and then broke the yolks to drench the potatoes. He then squirted some Chinese chili sauce on the side, which for some reason always brought on intense feelings of guilt. What would dad have thought about putting something foreign on eggs and spuds? Wasn't good old ketchup invented for that time-honored practice? Needless to say, he didn't know the answers to these disturbing questions.

While eating his breakfast, Sam thought back to when he used to be a bit wound up during the breakfast hour. He remembered the morning five years back when a guy walked into the Golden Coffee and ordered wheat toast with his scrambled eggs and hash browns. This drove Sam into an uncontrollable rage, for in San Francisco no one eats anything but sourdough toast at breakfast. So he muscled the wimp outside and pistol-whipped him on the sidewalk in front of the restaurant and its patrons. Unfortunately, the cops didn't see breakfast the same way Sam did and he had to undergo a lengthy course in Anger Management in lieu of time spent in the slammer.

Sam had since learned to somewhat control his rage, especially when others ordered their breakfasts. However, on this morning the guy that sat next to him at the counter asked for a white omelet with brown rice, dry whole grain toast, and a non-fat double latte. Sam's hand began to tremble as he reached for his gun while thinking: "Nobody orders that kind of sissified breakfast around Sam Marlowe." Then he remembered to repeat his mantra from the course: "To each his own breakfast!... To each his own breakfast!... To each his own breakfast!" And after several deep breathes, he finished his meal along with two refills of high-octane coffee.

As he sipped the final dregs out of his third cup, Sam gave thought to what had happened to the American breakfast hour, at least in *his* city. Shockingly, a typical San Francisco breakfast now consisted of a cup of gladiola sunshine tea and a bowl of mashed birdseed. If especially hungry, that was often followed by a medley of organic tropical fruits and a seventeen-grain croissant. Sam realized that any day a Yank needed to start out with a food invented by the French was a sad one for America, and it didn't bode well for the future of the nation.

However, Sam also realized that there was something missing from *his* breakfast? That missing, but most important ingredient was of course Babe, or some other farmyard animal. As well, he knew that more than just a few questions should be raised with the government concerning the modern American sausage, that is, if something manufactured from dried-up turkey droppings even deserved the name sausage. How did a sausage come to be without the help of a swine? What skewed sense of barnyard husbandry brought about this strange convolution and debauchery of the good old sausage? And the bastards had performed the same alchemy on good old bacon. Why, in San Francisco Sam had even seen fish sausages. How the hell did some stinkin' fish turn into a sausage? What violation of the laws of Nature and God Almighty warranted such gastronomic insanity? His dad was right to die from heart disease, lung cancer and cirrhosis of the liver in his early fifties, thus never seeing what happened to the country.

Fortunately, Sam took comfort when he thought back to the enjoyment of having breakfast with his dad as a kid. He used to watch Sam senior easily work through six ranch-style fried eggs dripping in grease, a dozen suckling pork sausages, a pound of smoked bacon, two or three spuds-worth of hash browns drenched in lard, half a loaf of toast soaking in real butter, and if the craving persisted, maybe a breakfast steak or two. All that fine food was washed down with a pot of good old-fashioned coffee, not some prissy-assed blend of macadamia nuts, Irish cream and lotus petals.

A Classless Collage in Union Square

After breakfast, Sam's head was whirling with thoughts about the workday as he walked south on Leavenworth to Geary Street. As was his daily ritual, he marched east on Geary and eventually past the Geary Theatre at 415 Geary Street, where years before his dad waited to meet with Joel Cairo. He continued along Geary to Lefty O'Doul's at 333 Geary Street, just west of Union Square. And feeling the need for another cuppa, Sam dropped into San Francisco's most-celebrated sports bar.

Lefty O'Doul's Restaurant and Cocktail Lounge was opened in 1958 by Francis "Lefty" O'Doul, a native San Franciscan. At the beginning of his career, Lefty played outfield in the old Pacific Coast League. He then played the same position for the New York Giants, with whom he registered a staggering .398 batting average in 1929. Sam enjoyed sitting in the sports bar, with its many photos reminding him of the days when men were men, and so were the women. However, this morning as he sat near the window overlooking Union Square up the street, he thought back to a very unsettling case.

On May 7, 2011, Sam read in *The Wall Street Journal* the thoughts of the writer and sometime San Francisco resident, Danielle Steele: "San Francisco is a great city to raise children, but I was very happy to leave it.... There's no style, nobody dresses up - you can't be chic there. It's all shorts and hiking boots and Tevas - it's as if everyone is dressed to go on a camping trip. I don't think people really care how they look there; and I look like a mess when I'm there, too."

Her astute observation gave him the idea of investigating where proper attire and social manners had disappeared to in San Francisco. He called his investigation, "The Case of the Snobby Sleuth," with his report ending up something of a diary:

I recorded my observations every afternoon when it was my regular habit to sit in Union Square. And just like the philosopher in Denis Diderot's *Rameau's Nephew*: "I can be seen, all by myself, dreaming on [Herb Caen's] bench. I discuss with myself questions of politics, love, taste, or philosophy. I let my mind rove wantonly, give it free rein to follow any idea, wise or mad, that may come uppermost."

Sometimes I walked down to Market Street, where the American deficiency in social refinement was forever and tragically being displayed on a daily basis. I often strolled about the renovated San Francisco Centre, the spelling of which indicated to me that only those of a certain English sophistication and genteel upbringing should ever contemplate shopping there. But I noticed that in practice nothing was further from the truth, for that architecturally stunning emporium was inundated with all the low-class Jerry Springer rejects that plagued every other mall in America.

At times like that I remembered a bygone era when "retail therapy" wasn't a hostile encounter with deafening techno music forever reverberating in the ears, but was instead a pleasant experience with the soothing strains of a Baroque concerto flowing through one's mind. And I remembered when shop-girls knew their place and only spoke when spoken to, and when shoppers left their flea-infested dogs and overly-large baby carriages, with weeping brats, at home. And I remembered when shoppers took some notice of their dress before being seen in public, and when they knew how to sit and eat in a proper restaurant, not a food court, which was the urban equivalent of a rural pig trough. And I also remembered when the underclass left the use of coarse language at the entrance to the mall, if they were even allowed to enter it in the first place, other than to deliver a box or two through a back entrance. Sadly, one can bring Bloomingdale's of New York to San Francisco, but one *cannot* bring its easterly class to the West Coast.

Regarding modern food consumption, local university researchers first noticed the compulsive feeding behaviors in society as they walked about the San Francisco Centre, where they observed what they thought were herds of North American buffalo, all contentedly grazing about the food courts. But after consulting with zoologists, they concluded that the buffalo was a much smaller animal. Finally, and with extensive research conducted on the subject, the scientists catalogued their observations and arrived at a number of startling conclusions.

During the modern mall experience, most shoppers graze from one snack bar to the next, never allowing even a moment to elapse without food being tossed down the gullet. Fortunately for consumers, the mall is ideally designed to encourage these sorts of compulsive feeding behaviors. However, the mall wasn't the only place where researchers observed the altered eating habits of *Homo bovine*, for they documented those changed feeding behaviors in almost every facet of modern life. *Homo bovine* could be seen grazing in cars or on public transportation, while on the job or in school, and during any sort of entertainment or shopping experience.

I soon discovered that the San Francisco Centre wasn't the only recently renovated place in San Francisco that forever lacked in class and manners. For every afternoon from my bench in Union Square I saw parade before me the shocking panorama that went by the descriptive "Modern Urban America." And every afternoon I saw parade before me the destitute homeless as they meandered aimlessly and panhandled along to the city's new official song, "I Left My Cart in San Francisco."

One wretched and pathetic man in particular often brought tears to my eyes, as well as pain to my heart. Every day he walked around the Square carrying a sign that read: "Stop Persecuting Me!" Poor, deprived and alienated from society, he sat down next to me one day and explained his heartbreaking circumstances, about the war on the American one percent, the rich. I was very much saddened to hear his pleas for help and understanding, and this from a man sporting an exquisite Armani business suit, Forzieri dress shoes and a Rolex luxury watch.

To comfort and make him feel less alone in the world, I offered him some thoughts of San Francisco bred Lewis Lapham from his 1988 literary gem, *Money and Class in America: Notes and Observations on Our Civil Religion*: "Attitudes of entitlement have become as commonplace among the sons of immigrant peddlers as among the daughters of the *haute bourgeoisie*, among the intellectual as amongst the merchant classes. Habits of extravagance once plausible only in the children of the rich can be imitated by people with enough money to obtain illusory lines of credit. As larger numbers of people acquire the emblems of wealth, so also they acquire the habits of mind appropriate to the worship and defense of that wealth."

Over time I came to the conclusion that San Francisco reflected more than any other city the rather disturbing direction that the country, and perhaps the world generally, was taking as it plunged headlong into an uncertain and uninviting future. I usually began my passing of societal judgment - an unlawful practice in ever so non-judgmental San Francisco - by observing the dress, if one could even refer to it as that, of the adolescents and twenty-somethings that called the town home. I quickly realized that the city was the very epicenter of the "Grungification of America."

I eventually came to realize that the general disregard for their appearance by the young was almost worthy of my esteem, for who would have thought that anyone not living through the Great Depression could take pride in wearing such an array of dilapidated clothing. And the concept of wearing the crotch of one's pants at the knee - simply because some high school dropout instructed one to do so - and waddling down the street like an inebriated duck was almost beyond belief.

One day I noticed a flock of young women flaunting their midriffs, which on most American girls over the age of thirteen were badly swollen to Biblical proportions. Without a doubt, there was almost no adolescent girl left in America that could or should wear a midriff top, for the flesh of life rather oozed over the edge, reminding one of a muffin-top. I noted to myself that perhaps the Kingston Trio should record a new song: "Where Have All the Mirrors Gone?" And even more pathetic was the sight of middle-aged or pregnant women flaunting their dry, patchy and marked midriffs, a sight that only the British could properly describe: "Mutton dressed as lamb."

As if their dress wasn't bad enough, I observed that the young of America also added a few accessories to make their appearances look even more like the starving peasants of Third World countries. I found it quite repulsive the use of rings to pierce any part of the face, an addition that made the more attractive ones appear ridiculous and the less attractive ones appear grotesque. And the thought of creating holes in the ears as large as a quarter, this stuck me quite beyond the pale and a practice that should only be acceptable amongst the poor wretches of a famished African tribe.

I also scrutinized the ever-present tattoos, which admittedly once looked manly on a seaman that had courageously sailed the high seas or on a soldier that had bravely fought for his country. But now, even women were proud to cover their entire hides with this so-called "body-art," otherwise known by discerning souls as a "tramp stamp." With this in mind, I appreciated all the more a thought of the French Prime Minister, Georges Clemenceau: "America is the only nation in history which miraculously has gone directly from barbarism to degeneration without the usual interval of civilization."

Along with observing their rather horrid general appearance, I also listened in on the intimate conversations of the so-called future of America. Needless to say, it was a mind-numbing pastime that often resulted in my wishing for the end of the world... immediately. For if couples weren't both rudely listening to music on different mePods or both speaking to distant others on different mePhones, the Latte-ites were searching Facebook for the absurd ruminations emanating from their ever-twittering minds.

One afternoon I listened in on a supercilious woman who was reading to a friend a new addition to her site on Facebook: "I enjoy sipping port in Seville." Unfortunately, this rather misinformed thing had probably never been to Seville, otherwise she would have hopefully known that one sips sherry in Seville and one sips port in Oporto, which is a town located to the north of Lisbon, not even in Spain. Needless to say, after hearing this nonsensical thought I appreciated all the more the words of Charles Luckman, who was undoubtedly correct when he observed: "The trouble with America is that there are far too many wide open spaces surrounded by teeth."

On another day I overheard a rather cognitively limited young man attempting to piece together elements of the English language so as to communicate with someone on Twitter. It was at that moment that I realized why that particular technological novelty only allowed messages of at most 140 characters. Given the general verbal illiteracy prevalent in youth today, most of the users of that questionable innovation are barely able to string together a thought worthy of 140 characters, and even that is undoubtedly a challenge. If the truth be known, members of Generation T, for Tweet, could get by remarkably well on a couple of dozen characters, perhaps fewer.

Over time I came to the conclusion that linguistic facility in using the English language was no barrier at all to communication these days. All one merely needed to do was take photos, in particular, of the variety known as "selfies."

Of course it probably had never occurred to most of today's narcissistic urbanites that there was once a time when photos were taken of only those individuals who'd accomplished something for the betterment of society, thus advancing the human race. And with that in mind, for those who were under the impression that they should take a photo of themselves and send it out to the world, I wrote a little ditty in Union Square one afternoon for them to sing. I called it *The Selfy Song*, and it's sung to the tune of *Frère Jacques*:

I am special, I am special;
Look at me, look at me;
Everybody love me, everybody love me;
Look at me, look at me.

I actually visited one of those websites one day, and it brought to light the excruciating pretentiousness of the members of Gen L and Gen T. After only a brief look at that vacuous nonsense, I wondered why those people took life so seriously, when it was so clear that life would never take *them* seriously. I could only shake my head and agree with an observation by Sigmund Freud: "America is a mistake, a giant mistake."

While observing life in Union Square I always counted myself lucky that it wasn't the Sunday of the annual Women's Marathon, an unfortunate city event that gathers twits there at the loathsome hour of five in the morning, a time when civilized folks are just getting home. If that isn't bad enough, an hour later and just before the start of the race, the national anthem is played, making sleep impossible within a dozen blocks of the Square. And when the lyrics "land of the free" ring out, the assembled crowd cheers mightily... hoping beyond hope that a multitude of voices raised in a deafening din will drown out the nagging inner voice that is forever saying: "Please release me from this unbearable prison of isolation that is my mind."

To add to this irksome urban hullabaloo, the never-ending reverberations of techno music are accompanied by some jackass who repeats over and over again: "Hello San Francisco, are you ready to make history?" Does this oblivious ninny imagine he's launching the invasion of Normandy or coordinating the Apollo moon landing? And what do all the "winners" receive at the end of it, nothing but a "Made in China" T-shirt and a "Made in China" plastic medallion. Needless to say, the only way for the multitude of hapless innocents in the neighboring apartments to get a full night's sleep is to focus forever on the ancient Zen koan: "What is the sound of twenty thousand cretins running?"

Despite my many disturbing observations, I never felt alone while looking down upon modern existence in Union Square, especially after opening the pages of an insightful book, *Mark Twain's San Francisco*. This collection of newspaper and journal articles from 1863 to 1866 paints a fascinating portrait of life in the City by the Bay, as well as of the folks that lived in town so many years ago. And not surprisingly, I learned that those folks hadn't changed all that much over the last one hundred and fifty-some years.

I especially took to heart Twain's description of San Franciscans from the June 26, 1864, *Golden Era* article, "In the Metropolis": "The birds, and the flowers, and the winds, and the sunshine, and all things that go to make life happy, are present in San Francisco today, just as they are all days in the year. Therefore, one would expect to hear these things spoken of, and gratefully, and disagreeable matters of little consequence allowed to pass without comment. I say, one would suppose that. But don't you deceive yourself - anyone who supposes anything of the kind, supposes an absurdity. The multitudes of pleasant things by which the people of San Francisco are surrounded are not talked of at all. But it is human nature to find fault - to overlook that which is pleasant to the eye, and seek after that which is distasteful to it."

After many months of observations, I came to the conclusion that some individuals in life are far more adept than others at seeking "after that which is distasteful." I came to this realization after learning about an English visitor to America by the name of Mrs. Frances Trollope, who wrote a charming condemnation of American's lack of proper comportment in a delightful travel book, *Domestic Manners of the Americans*, published in 1832. And her observations concerning the American people of her day applied equally well to many modern-day San Franciscans.

This wonderfully astute woman began her travels abroad in New Orleans in November of 1827, and from there she traveled up the Mississippi River to Cincinnati, where she settled for two years. What was fascinating to me, in fact remarkably so, about her account of this nation was how very little the manners of Americans had improved in the almost two hundred years since that dear woman's visit. For example, one of her first observations was of a most disgusting San Franciscan habit: "I hardly know any annoyance so deeply repugnant to English feelings, as the incessant, remorseless spitting of Americans."

Of all the Western nations, only in America is the practice of spitting acceptable, even amongst the supposedly better classes of society. Certainly the habit of spitting is on constant display by the groveling peasants of the Third World, and also by those of them that wander unhindered into the First and Second Worlds. However, only in America is this disgusting habit still practiced by graduates of better universities, which nowadays instill neither knowledge nor manners, but only the pecuniary training necessary to successfully accumulate capital in the modern marketplace.

Coming as no surprise, I learned that Mrs. Trollope's complaints concerning American manners didn't end with spitting, but continued on to native table manners: "The total want of all the usual courtesies of the table... soon forced us to feel that we were not surrounded by the generals, colonels and majors of the old world, and that the dinner hour was to be anything rather than an hour of enjoyment."

Taking most of my meals out, I'd noticed that the table manners of Americans had improved somewhat in the intervening years, though not by a terribly great degree. For even in many restaurants of San Francisco, I'd observed individuals unable to properly use a knife and fork, or to avoid chewing food with an open mouth, or to dispense with belching aloud an incessant stream of gustatory noises.

Needless to say, I found that the eating behaviors of those people resembled less the refined manners of gentlemen and gentlewomen, but displayed more the dining habits of the bovine. And as I often quipped to myself: "One does not mind a cow joining a dinner party, but the animal should remain on the plate and not sit at the table."

Also needless to say, I agreed with Mrs. Trollope that it wasn't just the incessant spitting and the lack of table manners that insulted genteel feelings, but furthermore, the low level of talk around that table: "There is no charm, no grace in their conversation. I very seldom during my whole stay in the country heard a sentence elegantly turned, and correctly pronounced from the lips of an American."

As true then as it is now, I also agreed with Mrs. Trollope that most conversations revolved around one and only one topic: "... [I] never overheard Americans conversing without the word 'dollar' being pronounced between them.... This sordid object, forever before their eyes, must inevitably produce a sordid tone of mind, and, worse still, it produces a seared and blunted conscience on all questions of probity."

Lastly, I could only imagine that genteel woman's thoughts on one other matter concerning the San Francisco dinner hour: The incessant wearing of baseball caps and other commonplace sportswear at the supper table became more and more irksome the longer I remained in the country. A pleasant evening in a pleasurable restaurant would, inevitably, end up an insult to my senses. The sight of men who had taken little to no regard in their appearance and attire made the entire evening repugnant to those of us who had dressed respectably, and so removed our hats as dictated by a proper upbringing.

At the conclusion of my investigation, I took hope from the ending of Mrs. Trollope's travels in America. After those two years in Cincinnati, she traveled on to tour the American northeast before returning home. And once back in England, she gave great thought to what the future might hold for the ill-mannered people across the pond: "If refinement once creeps in among them, if they once learn to cling to the graces, the honors, the chivalry of life, then we shall welcome to European fellowship one of the finest countries on the Earth."

A PI's Office in the Financial District

After debating whether to have a third refill, Sam decided that it was probably time to get to his office. So he exited Lefty O'Doul's and continued down Geary to Powell Street, where he turned south and walked to O'Farrell Street. On the southwest corner of the intersection there once stood Marquard's Smoke Shop at 167 Powell Street, the place where Sam senior used to buy tobacco during a time when real men rolled their own. Sam then continued along Powell and past the now closed Herbert's Mexican Grill at 161 Powell Street, formerly the location of one of his dad's favorite eateries, Herbert's Grill.

Sam continued down Powell to Ellis Street, and then crossed over to the south side of the road. He then turned east and made his way along Ellis to John's Grill at 63 Ellis Street. In the old days his dad often had breakfast there, though now John's only served lunch and dinner. He next continued down Ellis to Market Street, then along Market to Montgomery Street. However, before turning onto Montgomery, Sam watched the hustle and bustle along Market, all the while pondering on another investigation from a few years back, "The Case of the Pervasive Parades."

The San Francisco chapter of Curmudgeons International, an esteemed group of thoughtful and caring though easily-irritated souls, asked me to investigate an unbearable situation in the city, that being the pervasiveness of parades throughout the year. Hardly a Saturday or Sunday goes by without this or that self-promoting group meandering down Market Street, or some other road in town, and destroying the tranquility of a pleasant weekend in The City by the Bay. Isn't the workweek already filled with enough swarming inhabitants bumping into and getting in the way of others?

The effects that these rather irritating celebrations have on the already dire transportation crisis and waste management situation are ones that appear to be ignored by local government. And to make matters worse, city officials actually condone such irksome behavior and even participate in the loathsome festivities themselves. Naturally, when metropolitan bureaucrats are asked by any circumspect curmudgeon what need there is for a parade, the answer is always that it brings money into the town. Of course, the fact that cash flowing into this rather well-off metropolis is really just a siphoning off of badly-needed greenbacks from some far more-needy civic entity located elsewhere is a problem seldom addressed by the powers that be.

Fair enough, when the Giants win a World Series or the Forty-Niners a Superbowl, a parade is acceptable, even to the most dubious of curmudgeons. For the fact of the matter is, in those situations the town's hardworking sporting atheletes have actually set a goal and accomplished it. And when throngs of people gather along a city street to celebrate the nation's veterans, well, that surely is a parade worthy of applause.

But when a drunken horde of individuals dressed in green or a whooping gaggle of persons attired in all colors of the rainbow or a nostalgic gang of folks draped in a dragon train march up and down city streets, someone must stand up and shout: "Enough is enough!" For what have these supercilious sods done to be deserving of a parade, except for having affiliated themselves with this or that faction of society.

With all that in mind, I was asked by Curmudgeons International to investigate the origins and history of parades in the hope of putting an end to this all-pervasive public nuisance. According to Merriam-Webster, a "parade" is "a public celebration of a special day or event that usually includes many people and groups moving down a street by marching or riding in cars or on special vehicles, called floats."

However, that definition does not adequately account for most parades prior to the last half of the Twentieth Century.

The first parade in recorded history is believed to have been organized and led by Julius Caesar, the Grand Marshall of the Roman Empire. He and his troops had only just returned to Rome after conquering Gaul, Britannia, and the Germanic tribes of Northern Europe. Needless to say, he'd accomplished a tad more than winning the World Series or a Superbowl, not that there's anything wrong with a victory on the battlefield of sport. But it must be admitted that Caesar set a very high standard for justifying a parade, one that has seldom been met in the intervening years.

The next great historical figure in the history of parades was the irascible Napolcon Bonapartc. Again though, "The Little General," who history tells us stood only four-foot-wuss in his stocking feet, controlled France and Spain, conquered both Italy and Egypt, and was well on his way to over-running the rest of Western Europe, Britain, and Russia. Now here was a man deserving of a parade, and he damn well knew it. Napoleon even commissioned the Arc de Triomphe in Paris for his victorious troops to march under. Unfortunately, it wouldn't be French soldiers celebrating victory under that arch, but the parading men of another nation.

For all his faults, and admittedly he had more than a few, Adolf Hitler did know the worthiness of a grand military spectacle. And to evidence his appreciation of martial displays, after conquering Austria, Czechoslovakia, Poland, and the smaller countries of Western Europe, he marched across the French border into the Rhineland to enjoy the quite intoxicating white wines of the river region. After imbibing in those libations, his military staff non-chalantly marched its troops into Paris, where for the first time since being built, soldiers did stroll under the Arc de Triomphe. Although the Parisians found this rather irksome, even they had to admit that the French army had not tasted victory since Napoleon's triumph at the Battle of Austerlitz in 1805, the last military success in French history.

However, after World War I, and on the other side of the Atlantic, parades served not only a military purpose, but also an advertizing function. In the Parading Twenties, the idea of beginning the Christmas holiday season with a celebration on Thanksgiving morning took root in cities across America, first on the East Coast and then on the West. Naturally, once televisions became readily available to the populace, those festivities actually offered two beneficial side-effects. The first was that the kids had something to do while mom endured the drudgeries of the kitchen on that frenetic day. And the second was that dad could sleep-off his customary alcohol-induced hangover from the night before.

Nevertheless, the change in the nature of parades that occurred in the Sixties and Seventies is what curmudgeons call into question. The fact that one has arbitrarily been born into this or that group, or joined this or that group, and is now deserving of a parade after having neither attempted nor accomplished anything of merit, is what old school cynics take issue with, and adamently too.

What regrettably began decades ago has now permeated into virtually every aspect of modern life, and needless to say, into almost every parade that society incessantly forces upon an unwitting populace. Rather than honoring healthcare, education, civic, legal, and business professionals with parades, the rabble instead pays annual homage to those individuals who, through lack of initiative, have accomplished absolutely nothing deserving of accolade. And rather than venerating scientists, technologists, engineers, mathematicians, and philosophers with pageantry, the mob instead pays yearly tribute to those persons who, through general idleness of mind, have accomplished absolutely nothing deserving of praise.

With all that in mind and my report written up, I made my way to Curmudgeons International's next meeting, which is held once a month at a different San Francisco BrewPub:

Beach Chalet: 1000 Great Highway at the western end of Golden Gate Park and overlooking the Pacific Ocean

Gordon Biersch: 2 Harrison Street along The Embarcadero and overlooking the Bay Bridge

Magnolia Brewery: 1398 Haight Street at Masonic Avenue in The Haight

Rogue Ales Public House: 673 Union Street in North Beach and overlooking Washington Square

Social Kitchen & Brewery: 1326 9th Avenue between Irving Street and Judah Street in the Inner Sunset

Southern Pacific Brewing: 620 Treat Street at 19th Street between Folsom Street and Harrison Street in The Mission

Southpaw BBQ & Southern Cooking: 2170 Mission Street between 17th Street and 18th Street in The Mission

Thirsty Bear: 661 Howard Street between Hawthorne Lane and Third Street in SOMA (South of Market)

21st Amendment: 563 2nd Street between Bryant Street and Brannan Street in SOMA (South of Market)

After settling into a fine pint of the amber nectar, I was pleased to see on display the organization's motto: "There is nothing in the world that is not deserving of complaint." Also on display was the group's local slogan: "So much to complain about, so little time." And after offering the assembled curmudgeons my findings on the matter of San Francisco parades, about which they were most appreciative, I enjoyed several more pints, as well as an interesting talk by the president of the local group:

"The pervasiveness of parades in San Francisco has but one solution, and that is that when curmudgeons, such as ourselves, come upon a street spectacle, they must immediately retire to the nearest BrewPub and wait for the disturbance to end. And if after a few pints of the amber nectar a heated discussion breaks out, then all the better. With that in mind, allow me to offer for your consideration 'A Short History of Beerosophy'.

"As you all know the pub is no modern invention, and Western thinking on the concept of beer has been going on for quite some time. Reliable sources report that the Egyptians and Babylonians invented beer, and there appears no good reason to doubt this fact. And truly, those good folks are fully deserving of our respect and admiration for their very fine creation.

"But a higher place of honor must be given the ancient Greeks, for they were the first to give meaning to the 'concept' of the amber nectar. It was those wise people who founded the study of 'Beerosophy', a subject that is today sadly neglected within the cloistered walls of most modern academies, though not necessarily by the students meandering through them.

"The first recorded thoughts on the amber nectar appear as an inscription on the Temple of Delpi advising that all men should 'Know thy Beer'. That was essentially the beginning of the Western reflection on this most extraordinary elixir, though the world had to wait some time before the arrival of the 'Father of Beerosophy', the old Athenian gadfly, Socrates. Plato recorded that on any given day the great beerosopher could be found questioning the young men of the city about the amber nectar, advising them: 'The unexamined beer is not worth leaving'.

"The Romans carried on the quest for the ideal beer, though surprisingly, history books seldom report that the great Roman Empire was founded on the consumption of the amber nectar. On the other hand, Edward Gibbon attributes the Empirc's 'dcclinc and fall' to the over-consumption of that most unsavory and unmanly of elixirs, wine. Gibbon believed that this change in Roman drinking habits was a result of the words of the military mastcrmind Julius Cacsar, who upon defeating King Pharnaces, announced over a cold and frothy one: 'Drinki, Dranki, Drunkum.' For those not fortunate to have benefited from an education in the Classics, that phrase translates: 'I drink, I drank, I'm drunk'. Unfortunately for the Empire, Caesar didn't specify which libation to consume.

"Because of that lamentable omission, the Roman Empire fell and an Age of Darkness descended over the West, with the Church now forcing tremendous quantities of wine on the unsuspecting serfs of medieval Europe. And their unfortunate stupor lasted nearly one thousand years, almost as long as the misfortunes of the Chicago Cubs. But it wasn't until the dawning of the Modern World that a revolution in beer drinking occurred, one that makes the BrewPub explosion of the last twenty-five years appear almost insignificant in comparison.

"Beerosophy soon found a new mind in René Descartes, who while pondering over the meaning of the amber nectar, proclaimed: 'Drinkito beerum ergo sum', or, 'I drink beer, therefore I am'. The Age of Reason was also resplendent with some of the greatest thirsts that the world of beer had ever known, with Voltaire standing out as one of the highest beer drinkers among them. However, that consummate Parisian started a torrid controversy when he asked the fundamental question: 'Is there a best of all possible beers?'

"Unfortunately, the angst-ridden thinkers of Europe remained incapable of solving that conundrum. Even Friedrich Nietzsche despaired of the mystery, and he could only conclude: 'Beer is dead'. After that, European beerosophers slowly descended into a deplorable state of wine-induced intoxication, and with it, the worst hangover ever experienced in world history. In reaction to that situation, the British, forever lovers of the amber nectar, sent Neville Chamberlain across the Channel to stem the spread of wine on the continent. And though he promised the world 'Beer in our time', it was too little too late.

"Across the pond, American beerosophers were late to the discussion, but fortunately, ready to drink some brew. They approached the problem of the meaning of beer in a more down-to-earth fashion, one that the common man could know and drink up. So nowadays, the pragmatic nature of the average American has come to view the question of a greatest beer as a pointless and never-ending one. And perhaps Will Rogers best summed up the American position: 'I never met a beer I didn't like'.

"I'll now end this short history of Beerosophy with a few simple thoughts. Whenever I'm asked the eternal question of my preferred brew, my answer is always that my favorite beer is the one I'm drinking at the time. For as the greatest of modern-day beerosophers, Homer Simpson, testifies: 'Beer is the cause of, and the solution to, all of life's problems'."

To conclude his talk, the president announced, "Now, let us curmudgeons enjoy an evening of beer and complaint. And keep in mind, before our next meeting you'll be asked to choose from a variety of topics to complain about, namely, cell phone abuses that take place on public transportation and while driving, or laptop abuses by pompous little twits who take up tables in coffee bars while supposedly founding a new startup, or photos taken of family and friends and other adults who haven't done a damn thing with their lives, or photos taken of babies and cats and dogs who haven't done a damn thing with their lives, or why the City of San Franciso refuses to flatten some of its heart-pounding hills, or..."

Almost at his office, Sam walked north on Montgomery to Sutter Street and the 22-story One Eleven Sutter building at, naturally enough, 111 Sutter Street. Years back the former Hunter Dulin Building in the Financial District commemorated the most famous individual that ever had an office there, that honor being a photo from *The Maltese Falcon* in the lobby's picture gallery. Once at his floor, Sam walked out of the elevator and down the hallway to his office. He stopped only momentarily to admire the business title on the window of the door, one that had remained the same for many decades.

Spade and Marlowe
Private Investigation Services
San Francisco Branch

Sam Marlowe
Private Investigator

Letting himself in, he walked past his secretary's desk, at least it was her desk until he had to let her go because of a lack of business in the PI trade. He then admired the three photos on the wall behind her desk, ones of Effie Perine, Samuel Spade, and Philip Marlowe, his mom and two dads. The empty space where Miles Archer's photo once hung was now slightly off-color compared to the rest of the wall, which had also begun to fade somewhat.

Sam went into his office and sat down at his desk, then swiveled around in his chair to flip the switch on the office coffee-maker. As was his ritual each day, while the coffee brewed he thought back to when his dad and Miles Archer first met Brigid O'Shaughnessy, who at first went by the name Miss Wonderly. His dad also comforted Iva Archer, Miles' widow, in the office after his partner's death. And as well, the office had seen Captain Jacobi hand his dad the wrapped black bird before he died from a gunshot wound.

With the coffee brewed and a cuppa poured, Sam decided to pass some time as he waited for the call from Tom. So he flipped over the page of his "Private Investigator Word of the Day Calendar," which indicated that he was to use the word "gat" five times throughout the day. Using the word "gat," a PI name for a gun, five times guaranteed that he'd successfully stored it in long-term memory by the end of the day.

With his "Word of the Day" still in short-term memory, Sam decided to really test himself using his "Private Investigator Word Cards." On one side of each card was a common English word and on the other were "hard-boiled" PI terms for that word, with the rules of the game fairly obvious:

Bar: Box, drum, dump, gin mill, saloon, scatter, speakeasy

Car: Boiler, bucket, can, crate, croak, heap, iron

Coffee: Java, joe

Criminal: Hood, Johnson brother, punk, thug

Death: Big one, big sleep

Defraud or steal: Buncoing, con, flimflam, glaum, grift

Detective or Policeman: Bull, buttons, cop, copper, dick, elbow, elephant ears, flattie, gum-shoe, hammer and saws, johns, law, op, peeper, shamus, sleuth, snooper

Dumb guy or fool: Boob, chump, mug, patsy, rube, sap

Drunkard: Boozehound, lit, out on the roof, put down, smoked, tipped a few

Friend: Bos, right gee, right guy

Gun: Bean-shooter, gat, heat, heater, iron, rod, roscoe

Jail: Bing, big house, bit, caboose, cooler, hoosegow, joint, jug, pen, stir, under glass

Knife: Chiv, chive, shiv

Liquor: Corn, eel juice, giggle juice, hooch, hooker, jorum of skee, shine, white

Man: Bird, bruno, cat, gee, gink, goose, guy, hombre, jasper, jobbie, lug

Money: Berries, cabbage, case dough, cush, dough, geetus, jack, kale, lettuce, mazuma, rhino, scratch, spinach, spondulix, sugar

Shoot or Kill: Blip off, blow one down, bop, bump, bump off, chill off, croak, cut down, drill, fog, knock off, plug, poop, pop, pump metal, rub-out, throw lead, zotze

Woman: Ankle, babe, baby, bim, bird, broad, chick, dame, dish, doll, dolly, girlie, jane, kitten, looker, roundheel, sister, skirt, tomato, twist

After testing himself with the card "Shoot or Kill" and scoring 15 out of 18, Sam next opened up his office copy of *The Maltese Falcon* to read the beginning lines: "Samuel Spade's jaw was long and bony, his chin a jutting v under the more flexible v of his mouth. His nostrils curved back to make another, smaller, v. His yellow-grey eyes were horizontal. The v *motif* was picked up again by thickish brows rising outward from twin creases above a hooked nose, and his pale brown hair grew down - from high flat temples - in a point on his forehead. He looked rather pleasantly like a blond Satan."

Sam then used the office mirror to contort his face so that he looked more like Sam senior, who'd enjoyed in life a much more menacing facial expression than his less than intimidating son. Tired of those exhausting facial exercises, Sam turned on the office DVD player and watched the scene in *The Maltese Falcon* where Joel Cairo, played by Peter Lorre, got knocked unconscious by his dad, played by Humphrey Bogart. Needless to say, he knew that one day he'd have to play this scene out for real. Sam then spent some time growling in a threatening tone his favorite line from the book: "Yes, and when you're slapped you'll take it and like it."

After pouring another cuppa joe, Sam opened up his copy of Chuck Chambers' *The Private Investigator's Handbook: The Do-It-Yourself Guide to Protect Yourself, Get Justice, or Get Even.* This PI guide offered him essential professional advice in several informative chapters: How to Catch the Cheating Bastard, Cover Your Ass, How to Prepare an Intelligence File, Protect Your Identity and Privacy, How to Discover Hidden Assets, Cover Your Assets, The Art of Surveillance, How to Shake a Tail, and Missing Persons.

Just as he finished the chapter on how to shake a tail, Sam's phone rang, with Tom on the other end, "Sam, I've got some information for you. The body of a young girl washed up on the rocks under the old Sutro Baths. You better get down here quick before forensics carts it away. As a head's up though, stay away from the Lieutenant. He already warned me this morning to keep you clear of this case."

"Thanks, Tom, I owe you one," Sam responded. "By the way, should I bring my gat with me?"

"That's probably a good idea, Sam," Tom answered, "but keep it well hidden. I'll see you down here."

Sam next called Cosette, "I'll be by in ten minutes in a cab. All I know is that the body of a dead girl washed up onshore at Land's End this morning. And look baby, don't bother bringing a gat."

Cosette asked, "What's a gat, Sam?"

"I'll explain later," Sam responded. "And by the way, wear a loose-fitting top. I'll explain about that later too."

Land's End and Golden Gate Park

A Dead Girl at Land's End

After picking up Cosette, the cabbie had her and Sam at the western end of Geary Boulevard within twenty minutes. Continuing west on Point Lobos Avenue, they were dropped off at the Land's End parking lot. Land's End is part of the Golden Gate National Recreation Area, which includes around 80 thousand acres of parkland, making it one of the largest urban parks in the world. Though once governed by the U.S. Army, the area is now administered by the National Park Service, which watches out for its 13 million visitors a year. The GGNRA is actually a group of parks that extends across San Mateo County and Marin County to the north, to also include several greenbelts in San Francisco, in particular, Land's End and The Presidio.

Walking along the sidewalk past Louis' Restaurant, Cosette and Sam switched to the dirt footpath that took them down to the south end of Point Lobos and the ruins of the Sutro Baths, with the area crawling with cops and a forensic team. Opened in 1896, the Sutro Baths was a privately-owned swimming pool complex once touted as the largest indoor facility of its kind in the world. Built by the wealthy Adolph Sutro, the San Francisco Mayor from 1894 to 1896, the Baths stood along the water's edge until 1966. However, shortly after it closed for good, a fire burned the place down, leaving only the dilapidated concrete walls that once separated the seven swimming pools.

As Cosette and Sam hiked down to the ocean's edge, he said to her, "The cops aren't going to like me sticking my nose into things down there, so I'll have to make a small commotion to draw them away from the corpse. What I want you to do is get as close to the body as you can and secretly take some photos with your phone. Also, flash those brown ones of yours at some of the guys on the forensic team and ask them how they think the dead girl got there. If they're

40

hesitant to say anything, wave those girls of yours in their direction. By the way, that top's exactly what I had in mind. Hell, if I knew anything I'd spill the beans to you in no time at all."

Cosette laughed at his compliment and replied, "I've got the idea, Sam, and thanks for noticing. A girl always likes to look her best."

Just as Sam suspected, a few cops, including Tom and the Lieutenant, stood aimlessly around the young girl's body while forensics went about its business. So Sam raced ahead of Cosette and approached the corpse, yelling that he wanted a few answers. The Lieutenant saw him and immediately blocked his way to the body, telling him, "Marlowe, I told you last night to stay out of this, damn it." Then, looking at Tom, he said, "How the hell did he find out we were down here? I want to talk to the both of you now!"

The Lieutenant walked about fifty feet away from the dead girl, followed by Sam, Tom and the other cops. Sam knew cops from his run-ins with them over the years, and he also knew they were quite predictable. Since flatfoots always followed behind whoever was highest up on the food chain, the crime scene was quickly cleared for Cosette to conduct her own investigation.

While Sam played the irate PI, Cosette walked nonchalantly over to the body and took a few photos from only a couple of feet away. A member of the forensic team saw her and politely said, "You really shouldn't be here, Ma'am, this is a crime scene."

Realizing that she had a classic chump on her hands, Cosette gave him her brown-eyed puppy dog look and responded, "I was just curious as to what was happening here. That poor girl, how did she get here?"

The rube was hesitant to say anything until Cosette, in her loose-fitting top, maneuvered herself close to him. He took one look at her girls and spilled the beans, which he did in great detail.

"Thank you so much for explaining all that to me," Cosette replied before walking off with a smile on her face.

When Sam saw her leaving the scene, he yelled at the Lieutenant, "Nobody tells Sam Marlowe what to do!"

The Lieutenant looked at Tom and said, "Escort this shamus out of here. And Marlowe, I don't want to see you anywhere near this case again. If you stick your nose in one more time, I'll have your concealed weapons permit revoked."

As Tom walked away with him, Sam shouted over his shoulder, "You know you can't take my gat away from me." He then said to Tom, "There's something fishy about all this. I think there's a connection between the killing of that woman in Washington Square last night and this dead girl. What's the word down at Central, Tom?"

"You know I can't say much about active cases, Sam," Tom replied, "but just between you and me, I think you may be on to something. I listened in to a phone conversation between the Lieutenant and some guy at City Hall this morning, and it got plenty heated. But that's all I know right now."

"Thanks, Tom," Sam responded. "I can always count on you to do the right thing."

"When I can, Sam," Tom said smiling, "when I can. And by the way, that was a nice job at pissing the Lieutenant off so that that dame over there could talk to forensics. By the look of her, I'll bet she knows more than the whole lot of us put together."

Sam smiled to himself and walked off to join Cosette. As they began to hike up the hill along the dirt path, he asked her, "How'd you do with forensics?"

Cosette answered, "I took several photos of the dead girl and got a good deal of information out of one of the guys on the forensic team. What a chump, all I had to do was offer him a quick peek at the girls and he spilled the beans."

"That's all it takes with most guys," Sam replied, "especially those brainy ones. Needless to say, they don't get around too much."

"And how do the girls work on PIs," Cosette asked with a smile on her face.

"Pretty much the same as every other guy," Sam said laughing.

The two continued up the hill to the main sidewalk above the Baths and then walked down to the Cliff House at 1090 Point Lobos Avenue. The first Cliff House rose from the ground in 1858, followed shortly by its second incarnation five years later. Adolphe Sutro bought the place in 1883, but after a series of mishaps damaged the structure, he built a new Cliff House in 1896. Though it survived the 1906 earthquake, that third incarnation burned down in a fire the following year. Rebuilt two years later using a more modern style, the fourth Cliff House lasted until 2003, when a restoration project returned it to its 1909 style.

The Cliff House today offers two restaurants, the more elegant one being Sutro's, the sort of place you take a woman to put a ring on her finger... or to take one off. Above the dining area is The Balcony Lounge, which presents Friday Night Jazz. The other restaurant is The Bistro, where Cosette and Sam decided to enjoy lunch and talk about her investigation. Once at a table overlooking the Pacific Ocean and Seal Rocks offshore, she ordered a non-fat latte and he a cup of no-nonsense coffee.

As Sam drained his first cup and flagged down the waitress for a refill, Cosette said, "Sam, I hope you've cut down on your coffee intake. You used to get so wired from the caffeine every morning. How many cups have you had today?"

Sam sheepishly replied, "Maybe two cups earlier, one at the apartment and one at breakfast."

Cosette didn't believe a word of this and so responded, "At least switch to decaf for some of those cups."

Sam thought: "Nobody tells Sam Marlowe what to do." However, he knew that if she wanted to, Cosette would always be able to tell him what to do. He also thought: "When it came to her, he was as big a mug as the next guy."

"And Sam," Cosette continued to question, "I hope you haven't pistol-whipped anyone lately. Now be honest with me, have you?"

Sam grimaced slightly and then admitted, "I haven't lately, honest, though I did feel like pistol-whipping this guy at breakfast this morning. You would not have believed what that wimpish ass ordered in front of me."

"I know how you can get, Sam," Cosette said. "Remember, I was there when you pistol-whipped that guy in the martini lounge just because he ordered a chocotini. You must learn to let people order what they prefer in life. Even what goes into a martini is not etched in stone."

"I don't know that I agree with that," said Sam on the defensive, "but enough about me. Show me those photos you took earlier and tell me what the chump told you?"

Cosette took out her phone and brought up the photos, which they looked at together. Since the body of the dead girl was badly beaten up by the ocean and the rocks along the shoreline, she brought up a photo of the twins that her dead friend sent her a few days before. After comparing them, both Cosette and Sam agreed that it was definitely one of the girls. Then Sam noticed needle tracks on the girl's arms and pointed them out to his friend.

The sight of those tracks immediately agitated Cosette. So to take her mind off the matter, Sam asked, "What did the forensics guy tell you."

Cosette collected her thoughts and then replied, "He told me that she was probably killed an hour or two before being dumped into the ocean out by the Farallones sometime after midnight. He thought that she was then swept to shore by the incoming tide and tossed up on the rocks."

"That makes sense, time-wise," Sam nodded, "for that would have given them time enough to drive the twins down to The Marina, put them on a boat, and motor out past the headlands."

"But what do you think happened to the other girl?" Cosette asked. "Shouldn't she have ended up on the rocks under Sutro Baths too?"

"It's possible that she will, maybe later today," Sam answered. "But it's also possible that she was swept into the bay, which means she might wash up anywhere on the north or south side of the entrance, along either headland. She might even be dragged by the tide under the bridge, which could put her almost anywhere in the harbor. We'll just have to wait and see."

Once their lunches arrived, Cosette and Sam made small talk, renewing conversations that had never ended from a year before. Cosette noticed that Sam had changed somewhat since she last saw him, and that he was more at ease with the world, less volatile, less likely to pistol-whip someone for their choices in life. And Sam, he realized that he still had a thing for Cosette as he gazed out over the ocean while listening to Antonio Carlos Jobim's *Wave*.

A Loveless Summer in Golden Gate Park

After finishing lunch, Cosette and Sam left the Cliff House, and then walked down the sidewalk towards Ocean Beach. Stopping on a bench to enjoy the view on a fairly warm day, Cosette said, "I just remembered, I've got to phone my mom immediately. I was supposed to drive the two girls out to her place this morning, and she's undoubtedly worried that I haven't contacted her."

While Cosette spoke to her mom on the phone, Sam took in the view of the surfers catching waves out in the water, of the beachcombers walking along the shore, and of the coastline stretching far south from the city. He then took in the western end of Golden Gate Park, an urban greenbelt covering over a thousand acres. Its rectangular design is three miles long, running east to west, and a half mile wide, running north to south. And to the annoyance of New Yorkers, it covers 20% more area than Central Park.

While looking over at the western end of the park, Sam thought back to an investigation he'd worked on several years back. And as usual, he wrote that one up, naming it "The Case of the Summer of Rousseau":

After spending the better part of a morning searching for clues in the Haight-Ashbury neighborhood, the most noted district for finding out information concerning music from the Sixties and early Seventies, I made my way to the fortieth anniversary of the "Summer of Love" in Golden Gate Park. The first such event took place in 1967, the year in which San Francisco became internationally known as a welcoming home to "your tired, your poor, your huddled masses yearning to breathe free, the wretched refuse of your teeming shore. Send these, the homeless, tempest-tost to me," along with any high school dropout, lowlife deadbeat, drug addict or petty criminal.

On the MUNI bus headed down to the park, I unfortunately sat next to a pimply-faced young man with a T-shirt on that read: "Jesus Loves You." While handing me the usual pious comic book, he asked me if I knew Jesus. I told him I didn't think so, but how was the name spelt. He responded, "J-E-S-U-S," to which I responded, "Oh, you mean Heysoos. He lives down the hall from me in my apartment complex. Nice guy." The young man looked at me and then got up and moved to another seat, saying as he went, "I'll pray for your soul." And I thought to myself: "Can you imagine how excruciating it would be to spend all of eternity with such a condescending bore?"

Given my rather skeptical attitude as regards the first "Summer of Unbridled Lust," there was an important reason that day why I attended the fortieth anniversary of that celebrated event. And that was the music of the rock band *America*, with the first line of one song in particular of utmost importance to the case: "I've been through the desert on a horse with no name."

For many years I'd remained completely perplexed as to how a musician managed to travel "through the desert on a horse with no name." Although I readily admit a profound ignorance as regards horsemanship and equestrianism, it always struck me as odd that a musician could travel by horseback through a desert and fail to find the time to come up with a suitable name for his horse. I mean, it's not rocket science. And given that he was cognizant enough to remember his own name, why not come up with one for the damn horse.

Needless to say, though again admitting my profound ignorance as regards the psychology of equines, I have to believe that any horse of normal intelligence and friendly disposition enjoys having a name, and that any mount would be quite reluctant to travel across a desert without having a name. With that in mind, for many years it had seemed clear to me that the musician who went "through the desert on a horse with no name" was a completely irresponsible miscreant, one who lacked the good sense to properly take care of a horse.

So to get to the bottom of this incident, I attended the fortieth anniversary of the "Summer of Unexpected Pregnancies" to find this neglectful man and question him, perhaps even pistol-whip him, as regards his rather negligent behavior.

After tramping down the embankment and onto the Golden Gate Park field on which the "Summer of Unceasing Nonsense" was taking place, I found myself in the wheelchair access area that had been thoughtfully set aside for many of the casualties of the Sixties. And it struck me as interesting that all those misguided souls, who forty years earlier had popped hallucinogens to get away from normal, were now all popping Ibuprophens to get back to some semblance of it.

Once settled on the field, I watched the event given the perfunctory Native American - or is it Indian, it's so hard to keep up - blessing by a group of local professional ethnics. It was at this point that I recalled a statement of Jean-Jacques Rousseau in his 1750 essay, "Discourse on the Arts and Sciences": "Scientific ideas often stifle in men's breasts that sense of original liberty, for which they seem to have been born, cause them to love their own slavery, and so make of them what is called a civilized people."

So it was Rousseau who delivered the rather preposterous notion of the Noble Savage: "The fundamental principle of all morality, of which I have treated in my writings, is that man is a being naturally good, loving justice and order." Before moving on with the case, it should be noted that it boggles the imagination as to where Rousseau could have gotten such an absurd notion "that man is a being naturally good, loving justice and order." Look around at the bulk of humanity, dear philosopher, or just observe Gen L and Gen T in Union Square.

Needless to say, the Sixties glorified the "People of Mother Mud" close to an absurdity, a perfect example of which was the musical *Hair*, a performance in which grown people living in a most civilized city - New York - ridded themselves of their clothing. Fortunately, the aging and sagging flesh of the leftover cast at the fortieth anniversary of the "Summer of Noble Savages" kept their bodies well hidden so as not to offend the festival attendees.

The "Summer of Ludicrous Sermons" continued with another act that Rousseau would have been proud of, for he once proclaimed: "We shall no longer take in vain by our oaths the name of our Creator, but we shall insult Him with our blasphemies, and our scrupulous ears will take no offence."

Yes, a brigade of bombastic born-agains paraded the stage to remind everyone that Jesus, not Heysoos, had yet to return. It was at this point that I began to realize how closely aligned are the views of the Loony Left and the Righteous Right in America, with more evidence on this peculiar association coming later.

The next act on the day's agenda, and luckily the only such act, was a group offering up a medley of folk-scare tunes, a form of music that almost single-handedly ruined the American sense of taste in song. Especially annoying in folk music is the dubious message about how common folks are so loving and giving, when in fact, anyone who's visited rural America knows that country people are very seldom open-minded and tolerant of individual differences. Needless to say, some of those simpler folks also forever offer the nation an unceasing barrage of the Holy Bible and the Gospel of Hate.

Moving on to more evidence concerning the intimate association between the Aquarian Left and the Cancerous Right in America, the next speaker delivered a message from Henry David Thoreau contained in his 1849 work, *Civil Disobedience*: "That government is best which governs least."

Though conveyed by a member of the La-La Left, are these not the very words so often spouted by the Ra-Ra Right? Naturally, I won't even bother arguing the quite obvious notion that modern societies require adequate bureaucracies and sensible regulations to maintain acceptable living standards for all citizens. Unfortunately, this is a fact lost upon the vast majority of Americans, whether Republican or Democrat, as evidenced by the recent and rather pathetic debate concerning government-run healthcare. Of course, "Obamacare," a completely ill-conceived plan, is hardly government-run. No, it's really a sell-off of public healthcare to the HMOs and the drug companies.

At this point in the day's proceedings an enormous roar was heard far off in the distance, a noise that increased in intensity until the Blue Angels appeared in formation overhead. One and all were reminded that this was Fleet Week, a time when the ever-so-right-on Liberals of San Francisco invite the drum-beating Conservatives of Washington to demonstrate the aeronautical skills of the military industrial complex over the skies of the city. But rather than hearing angry voices emanating from the crowd, as they would have at the first "Summer of Love," the hippies and peaceniks of a bygone era now cheered the flyby while screaming: "USA... USA... USA." And as Gore Vidal rightly noted in his essay, "The State of the Union," in the September 13, 2004, edition of *The Nation*: "We are permanently the United States of Amnesia. We learn nothing because we remember nothing."

As the fortieth anniversary of the "Summer of Vacuous Senselessness" rolled on, the Poet Ludicrous of San Francisco arrived onstage to offer another dimwitted message: "God save the Constitution and the Bill of Rights." Of course the fact is that those two documents - both now in need of serious modernizations - were written by many skeptics, agnostics, atheists and other secular minds of the Enlightenment. Apparently, that detail didn't appear to have dawned on the poet's miniscule brain. Fortunately, with the empty-headed orations now at an end, the remainder of the day was spent listening to the more memorable musical groups from Sixties' San Francisco - the Grateful Dead and the Jefferson Airplane, or is it Starship, to name but a few.

While leaving the "Summer of Undiminished Twaddle," I couldn't help but think back to Rousseau and his thoughts from two hundred and fifty-some years before. He was sadly mistaken when he said: "Ignorance is held in contempt, but a dangerous skepticism has succeeded it."

Without that most endangered of species - *Homo skepticus* - citizens of a democratic society get sucker-punched by the Left and the Right into believing the most outrageous nonsense. Of course if our university educational systems were to ever understand that two of their principal goals should be to induce learners to question intelligently and to think skeptically, the problem of identifying nonsense might be solved once and for all, at least amongst the better-educated classes.

The La-La Left and Ra-Ra Right will probably never understand that the multitude of problems currently facing the world won't be solved by hiding our collective heads in the sand and hoping for a Garden of Eden that only ever existed as a myth. To solve those serious and persistent problems requires that people, especially the young, educate themselves in science, technology, engineering, mathematics, and of course, philosophy, which unites all those fields of thought as one. They must then apply that education to the creation and application of pragmatic solutions, many of which haven't even been dreamt of yet.

A Serious Sister from The Wine Country

When Cosette finished her rather long talk with her mom, she said, "Sam, my mom's coming straight into town, though I didn't tell her about what happened to my friend or the twins. She won't be at my place until around dinnertime, so why don't we take a walk on the beach."

Sam thought this a good idea, with the two of them soon on the sand and making their way south along the shore. Once down around the San Francisco Zoo, they flagged a cab for the ride back to Cosette's apartment to wait for her mom.

Once back at Cosette's and while she made drinks in the kitchen, Sam sat on the couch that looked out on a view of the bay. He always enjoyed sitting in her living room, it was so much brighter than his and it made him feel relaxed about life. Cosette soon brought in the drinks, his usual martini and her usual whiskey. After making small talk over the glasses for some time, Cosette returned to the kitchen and made a second round of drinks. Just as she brought out the second round, there was a knock on the door.

Cosette went and opened the door to see her mother. "Mom, I'm so glad you came into town," she said while the two hugged tightly. "Go sit on the couch with Sam. You remember Sam. Let me fix you a drink."

"Hello, Sam," she greeted him, "I haven't seen you in some time."

"It's good to see you too, Yvette," Sam replied. "No, we haven't seen each other in awhile, business and all."

Cosette brought out a whiskey for her mom and sat on the chair next to the couch. She then said, "Mom, I've got some bad news for you, but I don't want you to get hysterical or anything. About the two twins I was going to drive up to your house for safety, there's been a problem. Last night in Washington Square my friend, who was bringing me the girls, was shot and killed by someone. He pushed the two girls into his car and drove off."

"Oh, Cosette, that's horrible," responded Yvette starting to break down. "You sent me the photos of those two girls. They looked so innocent and so young. I wonder if they weren't underage."

"Mom, that's not the worst of it," continued Cosette. "One of the twins washed up on the rocks under Sutro Baths this morning. Sam and I were down there earlier and we identified her body."

"What happened to the other girl?" Yvette asked.

"She's still missing," Cosette answered. "But Sam thinks she'll show up somewhere around the bay over the next few days. We just have to wait and see."

"What are the police doing about this?" Yvette inquired looking in Sam's direction.

"Well, Yvette," Sam replied, "the cops are playing this one as if the killing of Cosette's friend last night in the Square and the death of the girl this morning at the Baths aren't connected to each other. I think there's a cover-up in the works, but I've no other information to go on. However, I do have a friend over at Central who's going to call me when he knows something. If he doesn't come up with anything, I'll have to look into things myself."

"I'm so glad you're here, Mom," Cosette said. "I knew that if I told you over the phone you'd fall to pieces. But don't worry, Sam knows what to do."

Sam added, "Actually, ladies, if I have to pursue this case myself, I'm going to need the two of you to help me with it." Looking at Cosette, he continued, "Since you have first-hand experience and connections in the exotic dancing community, you may have to contact some of your old friends. But at this point, let's just wait and see what happens."

"No problem, Sam," Cosette said, "just keep us informed about what you want us to do. Now, I'm sure we're all famished, so let me go into the kitchen and prepare something for us."

"No, Cosette," Sam interjected, "it's been too long a day for you to bother with cooking anything. Why don't I head up to Pellegrini's and order a couple of pies, say one vegi and one meaty."

"Good idea, and thanks, Sam," Cosette agreed. "I'll toss a salad and open a couple bottles of wine, Chianti for the two of you and a Chardonnay for me."

While Sam left to get the pizzas, Cosette and Yvette went into the kitchen to prepare a salad, open the wine and catch up on things other than the twin girls. On the other hand, Sam made his way up the street to Piazza Pellegrini at 659 Columbus Avenue. After ordering a couple of pies, he enjoyed a glass of Chianti at the bar and thought back to an investigation he'd worked on a few years back, one that he named "The Case of the Man Who Loved Pizza":

Once there was a young man that knew nothing about eating pizza, nothing about the various sauces and cheeses, and nothing about the many toppings. But one day he began to think about eating pizza, even though he'd never even seen a pizza. He quickly discovered that it made him feel very happy to think about eating pizza, despite the fact that all the adults around him said that he shouldn't think about pizza. Then one afternoon at school his teachers told him to stop exercising and to stop taking cold showers, activities that were designed to prevent him from thinking about eating pizza, and to go to the gym for a film on pizza.

Surprised by this sudden turn of affairs, he happily submitted to their wishes, though he soon regretted his decision. For the way they showed it, eating pizza didn't look appetizing at all, as it appeared to be a very bland food. Of course, after school his friends told him that there were toppings that could be put on pizza to make it taste much better. But since his teachers had said nothing about toppings on pizza, he suspected that his friends had it all wrong. And though he tried in vain to stop thinking about eating pizza, he just couldn't do it, despite the fact that he suspected that it was a very bland food.

Then one day something surprising occurred, with a pizzeria opening up right next door to his home. At first he was apprehensive about entering the pizzeria, but the owner was so friendly that he eventually walked in for dinner one night. And within a few moments, he'd enjoyed his first taste of pizza. Not too surprisingly, he discovered that pizza was a very bland food after all, with none of those toppings that his friends talked about. But since it tasted better than any other food he'd ever eaten, he decided to drop by for some more pizza the next night. Unfortunately, after knocking on the door he found out that he would never be invited into that pizzeria again, despite the fact that some of his friends ate pizza there any time they wanted to.

So the young man went back to just thinking about eating pizza, though his thoughts were now much more interesting, for he finally had some idea about pizza. Fortunately, another pizzeria soon opened up in the neighborhood, and this one offered a couple of toppings on the pizza that made it taste much better. And though he told the owner of that pizzeria that he would never eat anyone else's pizza, as soon as the next pizzeria in the neighborhood opened up, he dropped in to eat pizza there too.

The joy of going to lots of different pizzerias continued for many years, for each one offered new toppings to put on a pizza. One night he even went into a pizzeria and got to eat two pizzas, an item called *pizza à trois* on the menu. Of course not everyone he knew ate pizza, some of the guys in the neighborhood ate manicotti. And though the idea of eating manicotti sounded terribly distasteful to him, he did wonder in the back of his mind if he might be the sort of guy who'd also like eating manicotti. But after a while thoughts such as those disappeared, and he thought only of eating as much pizza in as many pizzerias as was humanly possible.

Then one day, and without any hint that something new might occur, he walked into a pizzeria and enjoyed the best pizza that he'd ever eaten. Naturally, he asked the owner of the pizzeria if he could return the next night for dinner, and he was assured that he would be most welcome. So he returned the next night, and surprisingly, the owner of the pizzeria had added more toppings to the menu. The number of toppings on the best pizza ever increased for many months, so much so that he decided to never eat at another pizzeria again.

For several months he got to eat as much pizza as he liked, and not only for dinner, but at every meal, and sometimes even for a midnight snack. And when the owner of the pizzeria asked him to move into the pizzeria permanently, he quickly agreed to the idea, even though his friends told him that it was a bad idea to make that move, at least if he wanted to continue eating lots of pizza. Needless to say, he didn't listen to his friends.

But moving into the pizzeria permanently was no simple affair, for cards had to be sent out and a huge party had to be arranged so that all his friends and family would know that he had moved into the pizzeria. And strangely, at the party a man who looked like he'd never eaten pizza in his life told him that it was now alright for him to eat pizza. He and the owner of the pizzeria then went on a short holiday, though unfortunately, only a couple of pizzas were brought along, and none of them had very many toppings. Needless to say, all of a sudden something had dramatically changed concerning his pizza.

Once back from the holiday, the owner of the pizzeria told him that it was time to move into a bigger pizzeria, though he had no idea why that might be. Unfortunately, he eventually found out why. For after nine months of only occasionally eating pizza in the pizzeria, and even then with very few toppings, a little calzone arrived and made the pizzeria too noisy. So he decided to work harder to afford that bigger pizzeria, one in which he might once again eat pizza peacefully.

After he and the pizzeria owner and the calzone moved into a bigger pizzeria, he found that not only was the family pizzeria not very peaceful, but that the menu offered only one topping. Even worse, every time he ate pizza another calzone arrived to make the pizzeria noisier than it was before. And sadly, he now spent most of his time thinking back on how good it used to be when he ate pizza in lots of different pizzerias.

Fortunately, one day a friend informed him that he should call 1-999-XXPIZZA. When he did, an owner of a pizzeria kindly told him all about eating pizza with lots of toppings. After a few months of enjoying that, another friend informed him that if he typed in a certain address on the PC, a whole lot of pizzeria owners would show him their pizzas with lots of toppings. Although it wasn't quite like eating real pizza in a real pizzeria, he came to enjoy his phone calls and web visits, despite the damage that they were doing to the balance on his credit cards. He also learned from a computer specialist that, despite what web advertisements say, there's no such thing as free Internet pizza.

Then something unexpected occurred at work, a new coworker opened up a pizzeria and told him that he could eat pizza there any time. Of course he felt somewhat guilty about even thinking of eating pizza at another pizzeria, but as time went on he could think of nothing else. So one weekend when he was supposed to be on a business trip, he instead dropped by the new pizzeria to eat as much pizza as he liked, and with as many toppings as he liked, just like the good old days.

However, the more he visited the new pizzeria while on business trips, the more he felt guilty about eating pizza there. In fact so much so, he eventually told the owner of the new pizzeria that he'd no longer eat pizza there. But after a couple of weeks of not eating pizza at the family pizzeria, and after having to listen to all the little calzones yell and scream every night, he took another business trip. And to his surprise and delight, he found out that he no longer felt guilty about eating pizza in the new pizzeria.

Then a few problems surfaced, for the owner of the new pizzeria threatened to tell the owner of the family pizzeria that he was now eating pizza elsewhere. So he agreed to tell the owner of the family pizzeria that he was going to move into the new pizzeria, but he never seemed to do so. Unfortunately, one day one of the friends of the owner of the family pizzeria spotted him going into the new pizzeria, and he soon found himself thrown out of the family pizzeria.

Of course as soon as he moved into the new pizzeria the menu changed, with only a few toppings now available instead of the many items that were on his pizza before. Even worse, the owner of the family pizzeria hired an expensive chef who demanded that large amounts of money be given for the upkeep of the family pizzeria and the little calzones. And when he saw that he couldn't afford the upkeep of two pizzerias, he returned to the family pizzeria, and for many months never enjoyed even one small slice of plain cheese pizza.

Then he read about something that might bring more pizza into his life, and so he rented a film that showed other people eating pizza. Unfortunately, the owner of the family pizzeria thought that he would rather be eating the pizza of the pizzeria owners in the film, and so nothing worked out the way that he hoped it would work out. But there was also another reason for the pizzeria owner's reluctance, one that he soon discovered in the bedroom chest of drawers. For sitting in the bottom drawer and all wrapped up was a huge plastic manicotti, one that he realized got to eat far more pizza than he ever did in the family pizzeria.

As the years rolled on, every now and then he went away on a business trip to visit another pizzeria, but eventually he found that his taste for pizza wasn't what it used to be. In fact, he hardly even wanted to eat pizza anymore, which didn't seem right to him. Fortunately, during the halftime of the Superbowl he was informed about a pill that would allow him to eat pizza for thirty-six hours straight. So without telling the owner of the family pizzeria, he took one of those pills. And that night the owner of the family pizzeria came to believe that he only wanted to eat family pizza again, not realizing that it was really only the pill that wanted to eat family pizza.

So he continued to take that pill for a couple of years, and he and the owner of the family pizzeria once again enjoyed eating pizza, though still only with a few toppings. Unfortunately, after taking the pill one night, and while only halfway through a pizza, an unexpected side-effect occurred, when his heart decided that he would never eat pizza again. And though his friends gathered together to say nice things about him, the truth was that they all knew that he was just a simple man who only ever enjoyed eating pizza, and that that was all that his life really amounted to.

Although he never knew the end of this case, the owner of the family pizzeria eventually received a huge check to pay for her loss. Happily, this paid for the calzones to all go to college, where most of them learned to eat lots of pizza and one of them learned to eat lots of manicotti. And the owner of the family pizzeria, she once again learned how to make good pizza with lots of toppings for all the young men who themselves were just learning how to enjoy eating pizza.

With the pies in hand, Sam walked back down Columbus to Cosette's apartment. Once the three of them were seated around the kitchen table, Yvette said, "Sam, you probably haven't heard that I recently retired from my job as a community college instructor. I could have stayed on a few more years, but to be honest, the area of Women's Studies has become far too political these days for my tastes. My purpose throughout my years in teaching was always to encourage young women to prepare themselves educationally for a career in their chosen field, hardly what anyone would consider to be a politically divisive goal. And though I won't go into any details tonight, the area of Women's Studies has changed over the last few decades and become politically fragmented and contentious.

"After quickly getting bored with retirement, I decided to do some research on the exploitation of women in the sex industry, perhaps even write a paper or two on the subject. You don't strike me as the sort of man who frequents such places, but the sex industry, or as some call it the sex trade, refers to any business that provides sex-related products, services or entertainment to adults. These products may include prostitution, strip clubs, massage parlors, sex shops, and pornography, either on TV, in theaters or in magazines. Needless to say, the list of these activities is practically endless.

"Of course, most of the sex industry is centered on prostitution, which takes place almost anywhere and involves sexual services provided to clients. These activities occur either in brothels or hotel rooms, and they're easily arranged either directly, say on the street, or through escort agencies. In some locales prostitution is illegal, in others not, though even in the latter, activities are subject to many restrictions. And though forced prostitution and prostitution with minors is illegal everywhere in America, a quick glance in the daily newspaper assures us that those practices are still widespread and practically impossible to stop.

"The area of the sex industry that occupies most of my research is the adult entertainment venue known as the strip club. I suppose this is understandable as Cosette in her early twenties directly felt the exploitation inherent in such activities, and we both now want to help other young women from being exploited at that very impressionable age in life. Research shows that strip clubs, or exotic dancing bars, make up about 20% of the legal adult entertainment industry. And there are an estimated 2,500 clubs, perhaps more, in the United States, with the industry increasing as fast as the economy grows.

"The popularity of a club is dependent on a number of factors: area location, customers' affluence, quality of facilities, cover charges and fees, and what's known in the trade as VIP rooms. Some clubs offer a nightclub or bar style, while others a theatre or cabaret-style. Though strip clubs mainly involve female performers, male strippers make up probably less than 30% in the clubs. And though a real gentleman would hardly condescend to enter one, the establishments known as 'gentlemen's clubs' offer luxury services, but always at a hefty price. At the other end of the market, bars go by various names: titty, pastie, skin, girly, nudie, bikini, go-go, as well as many other demeaning titles. Almost no clubs allow patrons to touch the dancers, though local laws do vary.

"The amount of clothing a female performer strips off varies from club to club, with a 'full nude' performer ending a dance with all her clothes taken off. A performer in a 'topless' club exposes her breasts, with the genital area remaining covered during the performance. And in a 'bikini' or 'go-go' bar, the performer's breasts and genital area remain covered throughout the performance. Of course there are grey areas between all three types of clubs, one being where the performer wears pasties on the nipples, exposing the rest of the breasts during the performance.

"However, it's the VIP or champagne rooms where the hard-core action takes place. One such routine, a 'lap dance', is performed by having the dancer rub herself against the customer's crotch area to bring him to climax. Another such performance, a 'peep show', is performed in two slightly different ways. The more common of them offers the customer a private striptease, but separated by a window, resulting in the man gratifying himself. The more expensive form of peep show is the lingerie modeling show, whereby the dancer strips for the customer, but without a barrier. And depending on local ordinances, private performances may or may not allow the patron to touch the dancer. In all of these variations, the amount paid is dependent on the type and the duration of the performance.

"Now, those are the performances that are advertised to the public. But there are other activities, very expensive ones essentially in the nature of prostitution. Judging by your photo, I'll just bet those two young girls were underage or close to it. They were probably enticed over one of the social networking sites, which is the usual way young girls find their way into adult entertainment these days. They would have had no idea that a career in 'modeling' involved something far more life-threatening. And once in the business, they were undoubtedly hooked on drugs by management, thus making it impossible for them to escape without outside help."

"You're right, Mom," Cosette exclaimed. "Sam and I both spotted track marks on the arms of the girl that washed ashore."

"Ladies, I'd always suspected this went on in those clubs, though perhaps not to that extent," Sam said, not terribly surprised by the conversation. "But look, these Broadway guys are ruthless and will stop at nothing to protect their holdings. We all have to be very careful and secretive, and that includes with the cops. Do either of you carry a gat for protection?"

Yvette asked, "What's a gat?"

"A gun," Sam answered. "But don't worry, without a permit it's probably best if you don't carry one. It's getting late now and we all need some sleep. It's been a very long day and I suspect tomorrow will be the same. I'll call you in the morning once I find out anything new."

Sam got up and went to the door, followed by Cosette, who hugged him tightly, which reminded him how very much he enjoyed being held by her. He smiled at her, then turned and left the apartment, but not before reminding himself, "Beware of this dame."

Downstairs on the street he flagged a cab and was soon at his apartment. However, just before he went inside he did a little calculating and then asked someone seated at the coffee shop near the entrance, "Sorry to bother you pal, but do you own a gat?"

The patron asked, "What's a gat?"

Sam responded, "Never mind, it's not important." He then opened the door to his apartment building, greatly relieved to have used the word "gat" five times that day. And for the next hour or so he thought about nothing but Cosette while listening to Chet Baker's rendition of *The More I See You.*

The Embarcadero and North Beach

A Pistol-Whipping on The Embarcadero

Sam was back to his usual schedule and daily rituals the next morning: dressed and caffeinated in the apartment, breakfasted and caffeinated at the Golden Coffee while not pistol-whipping any of the patrons for their morning choices, and delivered to work along the same route to the office. About halfway through his office rituals, Sam received a call from Tom telling him to be at Tadich Grill in an hour.

After finishing off the remaining daily rituals, Sam locked up his office, left the building, and walked north on Montgomery to California Street. He then turned east on California until reaching Tadich Grill at 240 California Street. Though originally a coffee stand in 1849, California's oldest restaurant opened its doors at many San Francisco locations before settling at its present site in 1967.

Fortunately, the lunch crowd had yet to arrive, so Sam easily found a seat at the restaurant's long wooden bar. The bartender had just set a cuppa java in front of him, when a familiar face sat down and greeted him, "Sam, it's good to see you. Thanks for working on that case for me." The former San Francisco mayor, a.k.a. "The Mayor," then ordered a coffee from the bartender.

"No problem, Mayor," replied Sam. "It was a fairly straight forward investigation. I hope your client was pleased with the results."

"Very much so, Sam," The Mayor said. Now taking a more serious tone, he continued, "Sam, I'm going to tell you something because you've done me several favors over the years. I understand you're sticking your nose into that Washington Square killing the night before last. As a warning, I'd stay well away from it. My contacts down at City Hall tell me this is a powder keg waiting to blow. Word's out that the police department has been ordered not to pursue the case. But Sam, since I know you hate being told what to do by anyone, just watch your back on this one."

"Thanks for the heads up," Sam replied. "Don't worry, Mayor, Sam Marlowe watches his back on every case."

"OK, Sam, I just don't want to read about you in tomorrow's *Chronicle*," The Mayor said as he walked off to join some friends for lunch.

After The Mayor left, and with a refill in front of him, Sam thought back to an investigation he worked on near the beginning of his career. That one he named "The Case of Mark Twain in San Francisco," with much of his investigation helped along by making extensive use of Twain's traveling recollections in the 1872 classic, *Roughing It*, and Albert Bigelow Paine's 1912 masterpiece, *Mark Twain: A Biography*:

Arriving in the Nevada Territory in 1861, Samuel Clemens first sought his fortune in the gold and silver fields. Failing as a miner, Clemens settled in Virginia City, where he wrote for *The Daily Territorial Enterprise* for two years. It was there that he chose what is without a doubt the most famous literary name in American literature: "... in 1863 I received word that an old and pompous steamboat pilot by the name of Isaiah Sellers had gone to a better, well, different life. And since he'd once used the name 'Mark Twain' in some long forgotten articles, I rightly appropriated that *nom de plume*. It's a river term signifying two fathoms or twelve feet of water, in other words, safe passage."

Needing a new adventure in life, Mark Twain arrived in San Francisco in May of 1864. He soon went to work at the *Morning Call*, gathering any sort of local news and then writing it up for publication. That sort of work didn't suit him well at all, and he even remarked about one of the staff: "Mentality was not required or needed in a *Morning Call* reporter and so he conducted his office to perfection."

Mark Twain lasted four months with the *Morning Call*, at which point the editor and he agreed that an early retirement was long overdue. To make ends meet, he then began reviewing plays for the *Dramatic Chronicle*, the granddaddy of the current city newspaper, the *San Francisco Chronicle*. In addition, he also contributed regularly to a couple of soon-to-be popular literary journals, the *Golden Era* and the *Californian*, which eventually allowed the name "Mark Twain" to become quite well-known throughout San Francisco and along the Pacific Coast.

Along with Twain, and as reported in his biography, there were an incredible number of talented San Francisco writers and poets that contributed to those two journals: "Mark Twain and Bret Harte were distinctive features of this group. They were already recognized by their associates as belonging in a class by themselves, though as yet neither had done any of the work for which he would be remembered later."

What finally allowed Mark Twain some financial freedom, which he sorely needed, was being rehired by the *Territorial Enterprise* to report on all the happenings around San Francisco. And with his newly found wealth and prominence, he wrote in *Roughing It* that he finally began to enjoy the many fineries of life in San Francisco: "I fell in love with the most cordial and sociable city in the Union.... San Francisco was paradise to me."

After Mark Twain's first stay of six months in the city, his fortunes plummeted momentarily, so he left town to take up residence and mining on Jackass Hill, over a hundred miles east of San Francisco. In February of 1865 he was back and broke in San Francisco at his usual digs, the Occidental Hotel, formerly located along the entire eastern side of Montgomery from Sutter to Bush. And around the time of that particular stay in town Twain completed and sent off *The Celebrated Jumping Frog of Calaveras County*, originally to be included in a collection of stories edited by Artemus Ward. However, the tale arrived too late for Ward's publisher and instead appeared in the *Saturday Press* of November 18, 1865.

That hilarious tale began: "In compliance with the request of a friend of mine, who wrote me from the East, I called on good-natured, garrulous old Simon Wheeler, and inquired about my friend's friend, Leonidas W. Smiley, as requested to do, and I hereunto append the result."

The yarn tells the story of a natural born bettin' man, Jim Smiley, and of his horse and of his dog and particularly of his bullfrog by the name of Dan'l Webster, the best jumpin' frog there ever was in Calaveras County. However, one day a stranger shows up in Angels Camp, and on seeing Dan'l he proclaims: "I don't see no p'ints about that frog that's any better'n any other frog."

Well, before too long Jim Smiley wagers a bet with the stranger, after which he takes off to look for another frog for the contest. In the meantime, the stranger fills poor old Dan'l Webster up with quail-shot. Needless to say, he's all of a sudden not the best jumpin' frog there ever was in Calaveras County.

At the end of that first Jumping Frog Jubilee, Smiley starts pondering on exactly what's wrong with Dan'l. In doing so, he turns his frog upside down and sees him belch out a double handful of shot. "Then he see how it was, and he was the maddest man - he set the frog down and took out after that feller, but he never ketched him."

After the publication of his tale, Mark Twain's literary career took off, though that wasn't until quite late in 1865. Although that year turned out to be a momentous one for him, the following year turned out to also be of great importance to his literary future due to a Pacific voyage to the Sandwich Islands.

Over the next four months, Mark Twain sent back twenty-five letters on the Sandwich Islands to an ever-growing and appreciative readership. By good fortune that voyage also served as the foundation for his first public lecture, one that took place on Tuesday evening, October 2, 1866, at Maguire's Academy of Music, formerly located just down from Montgomery on Pine Street.

Mark Twain was in no relaxed mood concerning his first public lecture. Such was Twain's concern that he even talked a number of friends and acquaintances into sitting in the audience and laughing on cue. Fortunately, his concerns turned out to be unfounded, and he got plenty of laughs right from the beginning. At the end of his lecture, "My Fellow Savages of the Sandwich Islands," Mark Twain offered his closing thoughts on his Pacific adventure.

Not surprisingly, the next day Twain got a good review in the October 3, 1866, edition of the *Dramatic Chronicle*: "On the conclusion of the lecture, after Mark had retired, the audience, as they rose to go, gave him a most enthusiastic recall, and not having heard as much as they wanted, called him for a speech.... Taking it altogether, Mark Twain's lecture may be pronounced one of the greatest successes of the season."

With the popularity of that first lecture, Mark Twain was on the move for speaking engagements in mining towns throughout California and Nevada, and he only returned to San Francisco once for a talk at Platt's Music Hall in November of 1866. After that, and as Paine wrote in Twain's biography, he left the city bound for New York by way of Panama.

Just then Sam noticed Tom walking in the front door, followed closely by the Lieutenant and the District Attorney. On seeing Sam at the bar, Tom motioned for him to join them at a table they were being seated at in the back of the grill.

The Lieutenant came at him first, "Look here, Marlowe. I've already warned you twice to keep your goddamn nose out of this case."

Then the DA laid in on him, "Marlowe, I have the authority to ask the Board to revoke both your detective license and your license to carry a gun. This case has nothing to do with you."

"You've tried to do that before," Sam said looking straight in the DA's eyes, "and it got you nowhere. Now I don't know what kind of game you're playing down there at City Hall, but I do know this. A woman was killed in Washington Square the other night and you're not doing a damn thing about it. I also know that a young girl washed up onshore yesterday morning, and I'll just bet you're not doing a damn thing about that either. All of us here know that there's a connection between those two killings, and probably another one, when the twin sister of the one at the Sutro Baths washes up somewhere in the bay."

The Lieutenant looked at him in anger and said, "This is your last warning, Marlowe. And keep your little tootsie out of it too or we may have to also talk to her."

Seeing red when Cosette was mentioned, Sam got up and yelled at the Lieutenant, "You damn well stay away from my friend and you damn well stay away from me!"

Sam turned and made his way to the door, with Tom right behind him. Outside on the sidewalk, Tom warned, "Sam, you better do as they say. This case goes way up at both Central and City Hall. I'm being watched too, so I can't protect you from them. Anyway, I've got my job and retirement to think about."

"I know you do, Tom," Sam said as he walked away. "But nobody tells Sam Marlowe what to do."

Still angry about the warning in Tadich, Sam hurriedly walked east on California towards The Embarcadero. While approaching Drumm Street he noticed what he thought was tail, a guy in a dark suit. To test his guess, he walked north on Drumm to Washington Street, then east on Washington to The Embarcadero. Stopping momentarily on the water-side of the thoroughfare, he saw his shadow on the other side of the street, confirming his PI's intuition.

Getting out his phone, Sam called Cosette and told her, "Our fears about the case are dead on, no one's doing anything and they refuse to connect the two killings. I just had another warning from the cops, this time also with a suit from the DA's office. You and Yvette better pursue whatever information you can get from your friends in the clubs."

Cosette said on the other end, "Yes, Sam, I've already made a call to my old friend Karette and we're meeting with her at five o'clock this afternoon."

"As a head's up," Sam warned, "these guys are starting to show a little muscle. So whatever you do, avoid being seen and watch your back. I'm already being tailed by some guy, though to be honest, he's the worst shadow I've ever seen. Anyway, I'll meet you and Yvette at Original Joe's at around eight o'clock tonight."

Sam thought he'd have a little fun with his tail now, so he made his way south on The Embarcadero to the Ferry Building. He enjoyed certain aspects of the renovated structure: the Acne Bread Company and its freshly-baked breads, the Boccalone Salumeria and its tasty salted pig parts, the Prather Ranch Meat Company and its nose-to-tail approach to eating animals, the San Francisco Fish Company and its California Dungeness Crab, when in season, and the Hog Island Oyster Company and its U-shaped oyster bar.

However, there were aspects of the Ferry Building that really pissed him off, such as the fact that he couldn't get a cup of straight American coffee. No, at best the shops offered French Roast, which forced him to think back on the cowardly actions of the Frogs during

World War II. He got so upset at this wanton disregard for true American coffee that he often felt like pistol-whipping some of the baristas. At times like these he repeated another mantra from his Anger Management class: "To each his own coffee!... To each his own coffee!... To each his own coffee!"

After reluctantly getting a cup of French Roast, Sam sat outside on a bayside bench and tried to stop his seething thoughts about foreigners. To relax, he reflected on when he used to join his mom there in the late afternoon of warm spring days. It was during those special moments that she enjoyed telling him stories about her part in solving cases, especially her help in "The Case of the Maltese Falcon."

As it happened, during that investigation Sam senior sent her over on the ferry to U.C. Berkeley to question her cousin Ted about the accuracy of the black bird story. As she was heading past one of the piers on the return trip, smoke blew over the ferry. The *La Paloma* was on fire and being towed out into the bay from one of the piers by the patrol boats. She always thought it was most likely Pier 3, given that it was a few piers north of the Ferry Building and that the prevailing onshore winds were generally out of the northwest.

The *La Paloma* was the boat on which Captain Jacobi had dinner with Brigid O'Shaughnessy, after which, Casper Gutman, Joel Cairo and Wilmer Cook showed up and asked about the black bird. Seeing the seriousness of the situation, Brigid agreed to a deal with the three, but reneged on it after leaving the ship with Jacobi. Suspecting that they'd been lied to, Gutman, Cairo and Cook returned to the boat to search for the black bird and accidently started the fire. Cook was then sent to kill Jacobi before he could bring the bird to Sam's office. Unfortunately for the captain, Cook did his job almost to perfection. However, Sam ended up with the Maltese falcon, as well as with a stiff on his hands.

After finishing his coffee, Sam spotted his tail again and so decided to continue having a little fun. He made his way to the front of the Ferry Building and then walked south along The Embarcadero, with Paul Desmond's *Embarcadero* now playing in his mind. After passing the bow and arrow artwork that he'd never been able to figure out, not that anyone else in town had either, Sam walked further along The Embarcadero until reaching Red's Java House at Pier 30. He decided a cuppa joe was definitely in the cards, so he ordered and then sat himself at one of the tables overlooking the bay and the bridge.

After finishing off a second refill, Sam continued south to the Java House at Pier 40, a place that first began catering to the needs of sailors and longshoremen in 1912. Finally shaky from his daily intake of java, and also now in need of some sustenance, Sam ordered a Baseball Special, a dog and a beer. When his order was called, he went outside and sat down at one of the bayside tables that overlook the boats in South Beach Harbor.

Sam was enjoying his dog when he saw one of the other patrons eating the other Baseball Special, a hamburger and a beer. Knowing that a burger on game day was completely un-American, his hand began to shake as he reached for his gun. He was just about to pull it out and pistol-whip the guy when he repeated another mantra from his Anger Management class: "To each his own special!... To each his own special!... To each his own special!"

Just then The Greek, the owner of the place, came over to chat with him, "How you doin', Sammy. Hey, many thanks for clearing up that little mess awhile back."

"No problem, my friend, it was an easy case," Sam responded. "But maybe you can help me out. Look over on the sidewalk and tell me if you see a guy in a dark suit loitering about."

The Greek looked around nonchalantly and then said, "There're a lot of people heading to the ballpark, but I think I see him, Sammy. You want me to send one of my sons over to move him on."

"No, that's OK," Sam replied. "He doesn't look too tough to me. By the way, who are the Giants playing this afternoon?"

"The Dodgers are in town," The Greek said. "Why don't you take in the game, it would do you some good."

"You know I think you're right," Sam agreed. "It's a great day for a ballgame."

Sam said goodbye to The Greek, left the Java House, and walked along The Embarcadero towards the ballpark. After passing the red and silver artwork that he'd never been able to figure out, not that anyone else had either, he walked further along to the 2nd Street Gate and the Orlando Cepeda statue.

Realizing that he didn't have a ticket to the game, he waved down a guy scalping a $20 ticket for $50. Walking up to him, Sam took out an old police badge that he always carried on him for such occasions, flashed it at the guy, and told him to hand the ticket over while making sure the chump saw his gun. The guy hemmed and hawed before giving Sam the hot ticket for the afternoon game against the Dodgers. Feeling a tad guilty at his little swindle, he handed the guy a double sawbuck anyway, while thinking to himself, "Everyone's gotta make a livin' somehow."

Sam continued to the Willie Mays Gate at the southern end of the ballpark, stopping only once to pay homage at the statue of the greatest all-around ballplayer ever, Willie Mays. He then made his way through the gate and into the stands to spend the afternoon enjoying a few beers, a few peanuts, and the sight of the lovely TV commentator Amy G. To complete a magnificent day for any Giants' fan, with the home team down by a run in the bottom of the ninth and two outs, but with the tying run on first, Posey homered to win the game. And Sam thought something he very seldom thought: "All's right with the world."

Back on The Embarcadero after the game, Sam walked north to the Hi Dive at Pier 28. He ordered his usual martini from the bartender, who said while putting the glass down, "This one's on the house, Sam. Thanks for taking care of that bum last time you were in. If I'd have touched him, the next day the punk's got my sorry ass in litigation with some damn ambulance-chaser."

"No problem," Sam replied. "He was getting on my nerves anyway. You know, some guys just can't hold their drink. But maybe you can help me out. Some chump's been shadowing me all day. Do you see anyone in a dark suit outside?"

The bartender went outside, took a breath of air while looking around, and then came back into the bar. "Yeh, Sam," he answered. "He's sitting all by himself in the outdoor area. You want me to shoo the fly away with a few carefully chosen words?"

"No, I think I'll take care of him myself, thanks though," Sam said.

Sam took his martini over to one of the windows overlooking the bay and the bridge, and next bided his time while finishing it. He then got up, said goodbye to the bartender, and walked outside and around to the outdoor tables. He sat down right next to the shadow and began talking to him in a soothing tone.

"Look here, buddy," Sam said to the bewildered man, "where did you learn to tail someone? You're absolutely horrible at it. First off, you must prepare thoroughly before shadowing your 'mark'. I can see you didn't do that. You also tailed me too closely, so buy some small binoculars and learn to watch your mark from a distance. Another option, purchase some 'spyglasses', which are sunglasses that have a mirrored inner surface so you can see what's behind you. Or another option, carry a small hand mirror so you can stand with your back to your mark and observe him in the mirror.

"Next, you want to blend in, so don't wear a suit if you're not in the Financial District. Be prepared to change clothes, especially if you end up anywhere near a ballpark. Even The Mayor wouldn't wear a suit to a Giants' game, though he might wear his fedora. Of course, I have to wear a suit as it's the only clothing I own. In addition, as I was walking towards the ballpark you were always on the same side of The Embarcadero as me. You should have tried tailing me from the other side of the street, that's what we PIs call 'paralleling'.

"Now, as regards the Java House at lunch, you should have carried on a 'fixed surveillance', or what we PIs more commonly call a 'stakeout'. You could have sat on one of the benches overlooking the harbor, perhaps pretending to read the paper. Remember, the idea in shadowing someone is to always blend in with your surroundings. Finally, I see you're packing a roscoe, that's PI slang for a gun. The cardinal rule is that you don't need to bring a bean-shooter along when doing surveillance work. And let me offer you one last bit of advice. Pick up a copy of *The Private Investigator's Handbook* by Chuck Chambers and let him explain all this to you, as well as plenty more. I'm confident if you work at it, you too can one day be a competent private investigator. Now, think of this as a learning moment."

The tail was so embarrassed by his learning moment that he lost his temper and grabbed for his gun. Sam knew this would probably happen and so beat him to the punch. He pulled out his gun with his right hand, and holding it normally, he pistol-whipped the guy with the base of the grip, striking him in a downward motion on the left side of his head.

Sam then explained, "You know, buddy, you gave me no choice."

Of course the man failed to hear his words, for he was already passed out on the ground. Sam next quickly searched the man's pockets for a badge or identification and found the latter with the name William.

Sam left the Hi Dive feeling a need for another martini, so he walked north along The Embarcadero to Sinbad's Pier 2 Restaurant at, logically enough, Pier 2. He always enjoyed Sinbad's, for it offered him an upscale view of the bay and The Other Bridge, an honest and unpretentious watery overpass, unlike the more famous expanse that claimed to be something that it most assuredly was not, namely "golden."

Once at the bar with a martini and a beautiful view in front of him, Sam gave thought to the proper way to pistol-whip a man. A common misconception is that one should pistol-whip someone while holding onto the barrel. However, this makes the gun useless for its primary purpose, which is to fire a projectile. There's also the danger of an unintentional discharge that could fatally wound the "clubber."

In addition, many handguns lack sufficient structural strength at the barrel and frame junction for use as an impact weapon. So, striking a target in this manner could cause damage to the gun. There's also a loss of time in switching from holding the barrel of the gun to holding the grip in the usual way. Of course, Sam seldom loaded his gun, but he knew it was always best to pistol-whip a man in the correct fashion.

Over his second martini, Sam also thought about how the proper way to pistol-whip someone had changed over the years. When his dads were PIs, guns were bigger and pistol-whipping was accomplished with the gun held in an ordinary manner. The procedure in those days called for hitting the target with an overhand strike from either the long barrel of the gun or with the side of the gun in the area of the cylinder.

Nowadays, handguns are much more compact, extending only around four inches past the trigger. This makes them much less suitable for pistol-whipping with the barrel. Instead, pistol-whipping is now best performed by hitting a target with the base of the grip while still holding the gun normally and striking in a downwards motion. This adds the weight of the gun to the force of the blow and uses the metal frame as the point of impact.

Just after seven o'clock, Sinbad's and Sam's martini began to shake from an earthquake, though it turned out to be only a slight tremor lasting about five seconds. Once the rocking ended, he realized that this was nothing compared to the October 17, 1989, quake that hit the Bay Area. And while looking out the bar window at the San Francisco - Oakland Bay Bridge, Sam thought back to the last "Big One" and to an investigation concerning that event, one that he named "The Case of the World Series Earthquake":

A few weeks after the "Loma Prieta" earthquake, I received a call from the management of the San Francisco Giants. The next day I met with them and was asked to investigate the possibility that the tremor was triggered by the Oakland Athletics' organization to un-focus the Giants' ballplayers during the World Series, which the A's eventually won four games to none. Since Giants' management felt that this was a most embarrassing outcome for the team, I was given the task of finding out what had gone on, if anything.

"The World Series Earthquake," as it came to be known, struck the Bay Area around five o'clock in the afternoon, just as the two teams were warming up for the third game of the freeway World Series. The epicenter of the quake was along the San Andreas Fault in the Santa Cruz Mountains, south of San Francisco. It measured 6.9 on the Richter scale and lasted ten to fifteen seconds, leaving 63 dead, close to 4,000 people injured, and 3,000 to 12,000 folks homeless.

My investigation into the causes of the earthquake took me down to the mountains south of the city, where I came upon several individuals smoking marijuana, which is not an unusual occurrence around Santa Cruz. They claimed to have observed in recent weeks a drilling platform erected near Loma Prieta Peak, though oddly, all the workers at the site wore Giants' gear. After talking with those banjo-players for some time and breathing too much of their air, it became clear to me that the worker's attire was worn to camouflage their true intention, which was to drill a hole in the ground, lower in a nuclear device, and trigger an earthquake.

After completing my investigation, I filed a report with the Giants' management stating that their suspicions were correct, but also with one recommendation. As it turned out, the A's attempt to unravel the Giants backfired somewhat, for the only part of the San Francisco - Oakland Bay Bridge damaged was along the eastern or Oakland span. With that in mind, my proposal to the Giants' organization, as well as to the City of San Francisco, was to obstruct in any way possible the re-building of that span of the bridge. In other words, it would be payback time for the City of Oakland and their beloved baseball team.

In consequence, due to constant political disagreements and petty bickering between the two cities, as well as the usual sporting ones between the Giants and the A's, the new eastern span of the bridge took 24 years to complete, twice the original time estimate, and it cost four times the original dollar estimate. Of course, I must assume that it was my recommendation for retribution that prompted these happenings, for otherwise there's no way to account for why it took so long and cost so much to build a damn bridge.

After downing his second martini, Sam thought about having another drink. However, given that the time was already half past seven, he instead left Sinbad's and flagged down a cab. On the way to North Beach he thought that it might be best not to tell Cosette about his pistol-whipping the guy at the Hi Dive. She always frowned on him doing that to anyone and it always caused her to nag him about his errant behavior. Sam knew there was no pleasing her sometimes, so he never told her about all his little accomplishments during the day.

A Secretive Sleuth in North Beach

While Sam was at the Giants' game, around three in the afternoon Cosette and Yvette left the apartment and walked up Columbus past Washington Square to Caffé Roma at 526 Columbus Avenue, where they decided to have an espresso and a cannoli. After enjoying the scene from one of the sidewalk tables for the better part of an hour, the two continued south along Columbus to Broadway. Turning east, they made their way to The Beat Museum at 540 Broadway, a place that both of them had wanted to visit after learning of its opening in 2003. Having explored the museum for some time, the two sat down to listen to a local writer tell a short history of the Beat Generation:

After World War II, a group of American writers gathered in the clubs and coffee houses of New York, forming what became known as "The Beat Generation." As a collective, the "Beat" community embodied certain shared characteristics:

the rejection of bourgeois and materialist standards, the embracing of non-conformist lifestyles, the experimentation with drugs and sexuality, and the introduction of innovative writing styles, ones often coupled with Eastern spirituality.

Jack Kerouac identified "The Beat Generation" in 1948, with the term "beat" coming to him from a conversation with a New York street hustler. Originally a Negro term for "tired" or "beaten down," Kerouac altered its usage to introduce a more jazz-centered meaning to the term, as in "upbeat" or "on the beat." In the mid-Fifties many of the Beat writers migrated to San Francisco, beginning what became known as the "San Francisco Renaissance." With the Beat influence waning by the Sixties, some of the less-intellectual aspects of the movement entered into the hippie counterculture.

Though not often identified by American writers, many of the attributes that characterize the Beats originated in Paris within the Existentialist movement in French philosophy. The concept of the individual alone in the world attempting to define himself on his own terms is common to all Existentialist literature. However, the coupling of the writings of Jean-Paul Sartre and Albert Camus with jazz influences occurred even before World War II. And the wearing of all black attire and berets was distinctly French in origin, with those styles undoubtedly brought over to America after the war.

In 1953 the poet Lawrence Ferlinghetti founded City Lights bookstore and the non-profit City Lights Foundation, which publishes selected titles with San Francisco themes. A year later Allen Ginsberg moved to the city, where he began writing *Howl*, a poem which two years later became the first controversial Beat literary contribution. Due to its graphic descriptions of drug use and homosexual activity, the California State Superior Court tried the manager of City

Lights and the publisher, Lawrence Ferlinghetti, for obscenity violations. Backed by the American Civil Liberties Union, in 1957 the case was thrown out, a judgment that helped to liberalize publishing laws throughout the United States.

Howl wasn't the only Beat Generation book taken to court, also charged with obscenity violations was *Naked Lunch*, by William S. Burroughs. A highly educated and prolific writer, he wrote semi-autobiographical novels dealing with his own drug use and homosexual proclivities. His third novel, *Naked Lunch*, published in 1959, was prosecuted in Massachusetts as being obscene, with the case not being thrown out until 1966. This was the last obscenity trial against a work of literature in the United States.

Of the many names associated with the Beat writers - Neal Cassady, Edie Parker, Joan Vollmer, Kenneth Rexroth, founder of the "San Francisco Renaissance," to name but a few - the most famous one of that numerous group was and still is Jack Kerouac. His most celebrated novel, *On the Road*, was written over a three-week period in 1951, during which he taped pieces of tracing paper end to end to produce a 120-foot long roll that was fed continuously into his typewriter. Written using a spontaneous style, the book tells the story of his road trips across America and Mexico with Neal Cassady in the late-Forties, with the work ostensibly about two young Catholic men searching for God.

Kerouac's first literary success was followed by *The Subterraneans, Doctor Sax, Tristessa* and *Desolation Angels*, all of which cover his travels in the early to mid-Fifties, during which time he often suffered from bouts of depression and alcoholism. Published in 1958, *The Dharma Bums* covers events occurring in his two disparate lives: his city-life of jazz clubs, poetry readings and wild parties, and his outdoor-life of bicycling, hiking and mountaineering. The recurrent theme throughout the novel is the main character's flirtation with Zen Buddhism, which Kerouac was introduced to in the mid-Fifties.

In the latter Fifties and throughout the Sixties the influence of Kerouac on the American literary consciousness extended to other writers, ones who wrote about the freedom of drifting through life and of experiencing the world in unexpected ways. The book even stretched itself into movies and television, most notably in the travel surf films of Bruce Brown, particularly *Barefoot Adventure* with its jazz score, and in the TV series *Route 66*, in which two buddies travel across America looking for a meaningful way of living. In fact, that show was so similar to Kerouac's *On the Road* that he thought about suing the CBS network, but was talked out of it in the end.

Kerouac continued to write and publish novels and poetry - *Mexico City Blues, Visions of Cody, The Sea is My Brother* and *Big Sur* - until his death in 1969 at the age of 47. The ultimate cause was an internal hemorrhage caused by cirrhosis of the liver, the result of a lifetime of heavy drinking. And like Kerouac, the Sixties also ended in that year, with America changing to embrace new ways of thinking... as it always does in the land of the road with the horizon far in the distance.

Noticing that it was almost five o'clock, Cosette and Yvette left The Beat Museum and walked back along Broadway to Columbus. City Lights bookstore at 261 Columbus Avenue sits on the southwest corner of the intersection, separated from Vesuvio by Jack Kerouac Alley. Opened in 1953, the store remains a place stocked with books devoted to progressive and alternative literature, whether in the small mezzanine balcony, the main level, or the basement. In 2001 the San Francisco Board of Supervisors designated City Lights an official historic landmark for "playing a seminal role in the literary and cultural development of San Francisco and the nation," and for its "significant contribution to major developments in post-World War II literature."

Cosette and Yvette made their way downstairs to the basement and Cosette found her friend looking over a book, *The Second Sex*, by Simone de Beauvoir. When they saw each other, Cosette and Karette hugged, and then Karette motioned for them to move to the back of the store.

Cosette said, "It's been ages since I last saw you. This is my mom, Yvette, though I think you met her years ago."

"Yes I did," Karette replied, "when I got worried about you and called her to come into town. It's good to see you, Yvette?"

Yvette hugged Karette, and then Cosette continued, "Why are we meeting down here? What's wrong, you look so nervous, Karette?"

In a hushed tone, Karette answered, "Cosette, that killing in Washington Square the other night has everyone in the industry on edge. She was one of our own, and that makes it too close to home. The whole scene has changed in the Broadway clubs since we danced together just after you arrived in San Francisco years ago. As you may or may not know, the sex industry is in transition right now. Even the businesses in Las Vegas are going under due to the economy and the ready availability of sexual services online. And it's no different here in San Francisco, for I'm sure you saw that The Lusty Lady recently closed its doors. That's really a shame, for it was the only sex club with its workers unionized, therefore somewhat protected from management.

"So with competition for customers increasing, the performers are being forced to offer more and more exotic sexual experiences or lose their jobs. And with places also going under, the girls have no choice but to perform them because the competition for jobs has escalated over the last few years. This is why we had to meet in secret down here in the basement, as I couldn't take a chance of you two or me being seen by anyone from the clubs. As you know, club owners don't like me poking my nose into their business affairs. In addition, it's gotten so bad that the girls are all getting distrustful even of each other, making the entire Broadway scene unsafe, with no one for the girls to turn to for help."

"Now tell me, Karette," Cosette asked, "what do you know about the twin girls? Do you have any idea what club they worked in and what they did there?"

"I'll tell you all I know, but it's not much," Karette replied. "I don't know the name of the club, but I did hear from one of the girls that it's owned by a guy named Gutt. The twins weren't on the main dance floor, but only in the most private of the private rooms. As you know, prostitution is easily arranged in those rooms, but it's only for the well-connected and the well-moneyed. Most of the gals refuse to get involved with this, but some always need the money to support their habits, which range all over the place.

"Now, rumor has it that the twins were contacted through the Internet about modeling jobs. They were then kidnapped out of state and brought to San Francisco to be used as private room prostitutes, probably after hooking them on drugs. I also heard that they were being visited by some official high up in City Hall, and that they were strictly for him. That's all I know, except that the killing in Washington Square may have been connected to the twin girls. Apparently, and this is still only a rumor, the twins have disappeared and no one knows where they are in town. Do you know anything about this?"

"What I'm going to tell you is in strict confidence," answered Cosette, "for it could possibly endanger your life. That woman killed in the Square the other night was a friend of mine and she was bringing the twins to me for protection. It appears that the girls were killed and then dumped out in the ocean. One of them washed up onshore yesterday and I identified her. The other twin has yet to wash up, but it's only a matter of time. The cops are reporting that there's no connection between the killings of my friend and the twins. However, I have a detective friend looking into the matter and he thinks a cover-up is in the works. And after what you told me about the City Hall official visiting one of the clubs, I think his theory is beginning to fit together."

"I need to get back to the Center now," Karette said, "but keep me informed about what's going on. We can't leave together, so give me a few minutes to get out of here." Karette hugged Yvette and Cosette, and then whispered in Cosette's ear, "I'm so glad the two of us got out of the clubs, it wasn't right for us at all. It's not really right for any woman."

After Karette left, Cosette and Yvette waited several minutes and then made their way out of City Lights. They walked across Jack Kerouac Alley and went into Vesuvio for a few much needed drinks. Just after seven o'clock, Vesuvio and the ladies' whiskeys began to shake from an earthquake, though it turned out to be only a slight tremor lasting about five seconds. Once the rocking ended, they realized that this was nothing compared to the April 18, 1906, quake that hit the Bay Area. So to pass the time, Cosette told Yvette about the most famous "Big One," a shaker that Sam had looked into many years before, and an investigation that he'd named "The Case of the Earth-Shattering Earthquake":

The 1906 earthquake hit San Francisco just after five o'clock in the morning, with fires quickly breaking out all over the city and lasting for days. The epicenter of the tremor was in the Pacific Ocean two miles offshore, and it's estimated to have been in magnitude between 7.7 and 8.2. The 42-second quake was felt in Oregon to the north, in Los Angeles to the south, and in Nevada to the east.

In the aftermath of the quake and the fires, 3,000 people were left dead and 80% of the city was destroyed. With a city population of about 400,000, the homeless numbered well over 200,000 and perhaps as high as 300,000. Though many of the homeless fled to Oakland and Berkeley across the bay, large numbers remained in the city at makeshift camps in Golden Gate Park, the Presidio, and the Panhandle, as well as along the beaches, with many of those camps still in operation two years later. In current amounts, the cost of the damage to the city is estimated to have been over eight billion dollars.

Though the 1906 earthquake is considered "The Big One," another "Big One" occurred October 8, 1865, one that was reported on by Mark Twain in *Roughing It*: "A month afterward I enjoyed my first earthquake. It was one which was long called the 'great' earthquake, and is doubtless so distinguished till this day. It was just after noon, on a bright October day. I was coming down Third Street...."

With their second whiskeys finished and eight o'clock quickly approaching, Cosette and Yvette left Vesuvio and walked up Columbus to Stockton Street, and then up Stockton to Union Street.

A Second Wave on Washington Square

Sam arrived at Original Joe's at 601 Union Street, across from Washington Square, just before eight o'clock, and once at the bar ordered his usual martini. The original Original Joe's opened its doors in 1937 on Taylor Street in The Tenderloin, though that restaurant closed when fire struck it in 2007. Five years later the new Original Joe's opened in North Beach, offering the same excellent Italian fare, and lots of it, that Joe's has always been famous for in San Francisco.

Cosette and Yvette arrived a few minutes later, and the three were quickly shown their table. After ordering the antipasto, a bottle of Chardonnay and a bottle of Chianti, Cosette informed Sam about what they'd found out earlier, "My friend Karette told us that the twins were being used as private room prostitutes in a club owned by a guy named Gutt, though she didn't know which club. They were also on drugs, but we knew that from the needle marks on the dead girl. She also heard that the twins were contacted through the Internet about modeling jobs, then kidnapped out of state and brought to San

Francisco. And get this, Sam. They were being used by only one patron, somebody high up at City Hall."

"So my hunch about a cover-up was on the mark," Sam said. "I knew those bozos down at Central were hiding something from me. That also explains why they've been hounding me about the case."

Once the antipasto and wine arrived, they gave the dinner order to the waitress: filet of sole - piccata for Cosette, linguini and clams in a white sauce for Yvette, and a very rare Porterhouse steak for Sam.

While sharing the antipasto, Yvette asked Sam, "What about that tail someone put on you? Was he any problem?"

"He was no problem at all," Sam answered. "I had a nice cozy talk with him, but he didn't seem to know whether he worked for the cops or a private party. Not a real bright fellow."

"Now, Sam," Cosette appealed, "you didn't pistol-whip him, did you? I told you I didn't like that sort of thing."

"Of course not," Sam lied. "I gave that practice up some time ago."

While the three enjoyed their antipasto, Cosette and Yvette spoke about what they needed to do the next day in order to research the case online. As they talked, Sam faded out of the conversation and thought back to a case he'd worked on twelve years earlier. That one involved an investigation into how the Dotcom balloon burst occurred so quickly and so devastatingly throughout the Bay Area. He called that one "The Case of the Troubled Techies":

My investigation first informed me that when not playing children's games, techies were doing their best to avoid productive work of any kind. In fact, most of them appeared to follow the rules set down in *Dotcoms for Dummies*, which listed a number of profitable maxims for helping ne'er-do-wells survive that less than adult workplace:

Maxim 1: At meetings, always keep the numbers of positive comments about other worker's ideas in strict accordance with the rank of each attendee. In other words, devise a linear or even an exponential relationship between job title and kissing ass.

Maxim 2: Never offer a solution to a problem that actually solves that problem. Instead, always formulate a Band-Aid solution that fixes the problem until the end of the day or at least until lunchtime.

Maxim 3: Never show initiative in a project, for if you fail, they'll never let you forget it. And if you succeed, they'll always expect the same excellent performance in the future.

Maxim 4: Under no circumstances should knowledge be shared, for if anyone else knows what you know - assuming that you know anything - there's hardly any point in keeping you around.

Corollary 4.1: Always feed erroneous information to co-workers, especially to anyone who may be looking to take your job away from you.

Corollary 4.2: Every now and then implement a Kissinger Strategy, namely, light a fire that only you can extinguish and then receive accolades for your save-the-day efforts.

Maxim 5: Beware of the woman who's always nicey-nicey, for she's generally the most malicious scandalmonger in the office. Also, beware of the woman who's always nasty-nasty, and that's for obvious reasons.

Maxim 6: If a co-worker dies and a McSympathy card is passed around for the much-relieved spouse, just sign it, for there's hell to pay if you don't show some false emotions.

Maxim 7: If clean-up assignments are posted for the office kitchen, don't bother doing anything on your assigned day. Needless to say, everyone is too busy to notice what's going on in the kitchen anyway.

Corollary 7.1: When leaving cups or dishes in the office sink for the office mother to clean up, look repentant if walked in on and then run a little holy water over them in atonement for your sins.

Corollary 7.2: Leave leftovers in the office refrigerator for months at a time, at least until a sign shows up claiming that everything will be thrown out on Friday afternoon. Then, save any leftovers in the supervisor's bottom desk drawer over the weekend and return them to the refrigerator on Monday morning.

Maxim 8: If childless, place a photo of someone else's kids in your cube. This is done so that any time the supervisor comes around looking for volunteers to stay late, the excuse is that you have to pick up the kids right after work.

Corollary 8.1: Always prepare an elaborate excuse, way ahead of time, for why the family is once again not at the office Christmas dinner or the Fourth of July picnic.

Corollary 8.2: When arranging for government-sanctioned family-leave due to your youngest daughter's pending operation and subsequent rehabilitation in the Mayo Clinic, always call in regularly, despite the fact that there's not a damn thing that you could possibly do while lying on the beach in Waikiki. Call in sick for a couple of weeks after you return from the islands, at least as long as it takes for your tan to fade a bit.

Maxim 9: Create a fancy spreadsheet with lots of incomprehensible charts, and then make sure that it can be quickly flipped on whenever anyone noses about while you're viewing *Yahoo! Sports*, *Golden Gate Fields* post times, or porn sites of any kind.

Corollary 9.1: To this end, install an early warning system for alerting the idle worker that trouble is on the way, such as a laser-beam that when crossed automatically closes out of the sites mentioned and brings up that fancy spreadsheet with lots of incomprehensible charts.

Maxim 10: If the boss comes up with a new project, tell him or her to outline it in an e-mail, for needless to say, the prospect of writing down all the particulars of the new project will guarantee that someone else will be assigned the work.

Corollary 10.1: As concerns e-mail, direct all of it into a *Whatever* folder, which is a black hole from which no information can ever again be delivered into the universe of the idle worker.

Unfortunately for techies everywhere in the Bay Area, management at a number of startups came across *Dotcoms for Dummies* and proceeded to develop a plan to run an office just like the hard labor farm in *Cool Hand Luke*. In that office, the CEO first announces to his prisoners each morning: "Now what we have here is a failure to communicate." He then continues his thoughts: "I can be a good guy or I can be one mean son-of-a-bitch." Finally, the CEO reads off his set of rules and repercussions to the inmates:

Rule 1: Leave copies on the printer.
Repercussion 1: A night in the cube.

Rule 2: Leave a coffee cup in the sink.
Repercussion 2: A night in the cube.

Rule 3: Don't arrive early to work.
Repercussion 3: A night in the cube.

Rule 4: Arrive late to an office meeting.
Repercussion 4: A night in the cube.

Rule 5: Leave early from work.
Repercussion 5: A night in the cube.

Rule 6: Read *Yahoo! Sports, Golden Gate Fields* post times, or porn sites of any kind on the job.
Repercussion 6: A night in the cube.

Rule 7: Don't read my e-mails.
Repercussion 7: A night in the cube.

Rule 8: Attempt to cover your ass.
Repercussion 8: A night in the cube.

Rule 9: Don't kiss my ass.
Repercussion 9: A night in the cube.

Rule 10: Fail to communicate what I want to hear.
Repercussion 10: A night in the cube.

Needless to say, the application of this workplace plan was doomed from the beginning and so enjoyed only a very limited success. For the ne'er-do-wells, a breed that has always greatly out-numbered hard-working stiffs, still remained forever underfoot. This of course shouldn't have been a surprise to management, for in 1875 Mark Twain wrote about idle office workers in a memoir of his newspaper days called *The*

Office Bore: "To have to sit and endure the presence of a bore day after day... Physical pain is pastime to it, and hanging a pleasure excursion."

Continuing with my investigation, I soon discovered that researchers believed that that office idleness might be due to the harmful effects on male vitality caused by the fancy typewriter, in particular, an alarming decrease in the testosterone level of males working in the Dotcom workplace. Realizing the implications of that health condition for the future of business, as well as for the future of society, they looked into possible causes of the epidemic. They found that there was a strong correlation between testosterone level and technology. Specifically, males working on a fancy typewriter were more likely to have decreased levels of the male hormone. In fact, the decrease was proportional to the amount of time spent in front of a PC or laptop each day.

In the non-techie control group, it was observed that males who spent no time in front of a fancy typewriter each day registered a testosterone level one hundred percent of normal. In other words, they suffered no loss of male vitality during the day. But as the number of PC or laptop hours increased in the techie treatment group, the percentage of the male hormone lost to techie working conditions became more and more acute. The most frightening aspect of the study was that after spending even one hour on a computer, testosterone levels were already down by half, and it only got worse from then on. And after four hours in front of the fancy typewriter, there was only a negligible change in testosterone levels, mainly because the vitality of male techies at that point was almost too low to measure anyway.

After completing the initial phase of their study, the problem was how to engender in male techies a renewed sense of vitality, thus increasing testosterone levels. Fortunately, ManTech, a Bay Area software development firm, offered a possible solution to the dilemma. That solution was "ManSaver," a screensaver designed to help elevate the testosterone levels of male workers by showing them scenes of men involved in hormone-producing activities: correctly operating home power tools, removing and reassembling the engine of a '56 Chevy, and grilling a five pound piece of succulent sirloin on the backyard BBQ.

Although "ManSaver" helped increase testosterone levels somewhat, researchers found that an additional approach was necessary. The answer was to create a new programming language to instruct male workers how to socialize with female techies. That revolutionary advance in programming was "Beer Basic," with one program written to help male techies get to Happy Hour each day so as to socialize with female techies:

```
**Declare variables**

VAR HappyHour
VAR Brew
DIM Brew(4)

**Initialize variables**

HappyHour = ""
Brew(4) = ("Lager","Ale","Porter","Stout")
HappyHour()

PROCEDURE HappyHour()

Get HappyHour
```

DO WHILE HappyHour = "Yes"

Get Brew(4)

Get HappyHour

END WHILE

END PROCEDURE HappyHour()

Researchers concluded that the point of Happy Hour each day was for male techies to actually meet and entertain female techies, which is, of course, the old-fashioned way of increasing testosterone levels. Although the research did indeed help accomplish this goal to some extent, as with any personal relationships, sometimes techies were in dire emotional need of tech support:

Dear Tech Support,

Last year I upgraded from Girlfriend 5.0 to Wife 1.0 and noticed a slowdown in overall performance, particularly in the love and affection applications that had operated flawlessly under Girlfriend 5.0. In addition, Wife 1.0 froze many valuable programs, such as NFL 4.1, NBA 3.4 and MLB 6.7. It also installed some undesirable programs, such as Conversation 8.3, Fitness 1.2, Headaches 10.0, Shopping 7.5 and House Cleaning 3.7. Even worse, Wife 1.0 forever runs Nagging 6.2, Tears 5.7 and Guilt 2.4, forcing me to constantly run Grumpy 7.5, Beer 5.2 and Pub 6.8. What should I do?

Signed, Desperate.

Dear Desperate,

Keep in mind that Girlfriend 5.0 is an entertainment package, while Wife 1.0 is an operating system. So try running Flowers 3.2, Dinner 2.7 or Jewelry 4.3, which should allow Wife 1.0 to occasionally run Love 8.4. Also, don't allow Wife 1.0 to install Mother-in-Law 1.0, otherwise your system will crash and you'll be forced to repeatedly run Happy Hour 6.7. And under no circumstances is it advisable to run Girlfriend 6.0, for that application eventually installs Wife 2.0, which means I'll hear from you once again in the future.

Good luck, Tech Support.

Naturally, San Francisco, as well as the rest of the Bay Area, needed more than just a little tech support when the Dotcom balloon finally burst, leaving so many techies without their dreamt of fortunes. Of course, this wasn't the first time that such a calamity had visited the good folks of this wealth-obsessed city, for Mark Twain mentioned his all-consuming madness and what happened to it in *Roughing It*: "Then - all of a sudden, out went the bottom and everything and everybody went to ruin and destruction!... I was an early beggar and a thorough one."

Years later Mark Twain reflected upon that episode, as well as many others, in *The Gilded Age*, published with Charles Dudley Warner in 1873. And as the subtitle of the book states, it truly is *A Tale of Today*: "They see people, all around them, poor yesterday, rich today, who have come into sudden opulence by some means which they could not have classified among any of the regular occupations of life."

At that point, Sam listened back in on the conversation when Cosette said, "Mom, did you see the article in the *Chronicle* the other day that was concerned with a local tech conference. Apparently, some presentations involved male masturbatory behavior and the mockery of female breasts. As if it's not enough that women in tech make salaries somewhat lower than their male counterparts, they also have to endure sexual humiliation from those child-men. It's no wonder that women refuse to attend post-conference social gatherings, which actually hurts their careers as that's where a great deal of business networking takes place."

"That's been going on for some time in the tech industry," Yvette added. "Though long a male-dominated profession, for decades the educational system has encouraged women to pursue careers in technology. However, once in the workplace, the problem is that male techies are threatened by what they see as an intrusion into their private, or should I say primate, domain. As a consequence, these child-men fight back through various techniques of humiliation, derision and harassment. And it should come as no surprise that if you go to any of the Broadway or other San Francisco sex clubs, especially during a city tech conference, they're filled with pathetically pubescent techies, with their bar tabs often picked up by corporate sponsors."

With their meals now in front of them and another bottle of Chianti on the way, Yvette began a new conversation, "It concerns me that with all the strides in the women's movement over the last sixty years that girls are still being used by men for their personal entertainment. Perhaps I was a bit naive, but back in the Seventies I thought this was all going away, that men would finally give women the respect and dignity they deserve. The champions of second-wave feminism must be shaking their collective heads at our current situation."

"Mom, I don't know that Sam has ever heard the term 'second-wave feminism'," Cosette said. "Maybe you better explain it to him."

"Well, Sam," Yvette began, "if you don't mind, I'll give you the first day's lecture of the Introduction to Women's Studies class that I once taught at the community college. As an ideology, feminism is a movement aimed at not only defining, but also establishing equal rights for women, whether in the political, economic or social spheres. In essence, a feminist advocates for the rights and equality of women, especially as regards equal access to a good education and decent employment. In this sense, every male who supports the equality of women is a feminist, though whether they want to be called that or not is another thing. However, it's always amazing to me how certain political and religious groups in this country are so threatened by something so democratic in nature.

"The term 'first-wave feminism' was coined in the 1980's, and it refers to the period of feminist activity that took place during the nineteenth and early twentieth centuries. The focus of first-wave feminists was primarily women's suffrage, in other words, the right to vote and property rights. With feminists speaking out all over Europe, especially in Britain, America too became an epicenter for feminist voices. Feminist activism was on the rise through the hard work of Lucretia Coffin Mott, Elizabeth Cady Stanton, Lucy Stone, Victoria Woodhull, Matilda Joslyn Gage, as well as the most well-known of them all, Susan B. Anthony.

"With most of the first-wave feminist agenda finally in place prior to World War II, the movement remained in limbo until the arrival of the second-wave feminist agenda: sexuality rights, reproductive rights, family law, marital rape law, divorce law, children's custody, workplace conditions, legal inequalities, and violence against women.

"In America, the first voice for second-wave feminism was Betty Friedan in her 1963 groundbreaking book *The Feminine Mystique.* At the beginning of her classic work, she noted that 'the problem that has no name' was the result of the successes of first-wave feminism, in that there was a loss of interest in the rights of woman in the belief that all had been accomplished by earlier feminists. But as she further noted, after the war and during the Fifties, women married at younger ages and had more children. And though women more and more went to college, after graduation they still worked in the home. As a consequence, mental health problems amongst women were rampant at every social level of American society.

"At the beginning of her work, Friedan addressed the nature of the crisis: 'The problem that has no name stirring in the minds of so many American women today is not a matter of loss of femininity or too much education, or the demands of domesticity. It is far more important than anyone recognizes. It is the key to other new and old problems which have been torturing women and their husbands and their children, and puzzling their doctors and educators for years. It may well be the key to our future as a nation and a culture. We can no longer ignore that voice within women that says: I want something more than my husband and my children and my home.'

"After an extensive analysis about how 'the problem that has no name' played itself out in American society, at the end of her book Friedan offered a solution, a new life plan for each woman. So as with other feminist thinkers, Friedan's solution asked every woman to define her own being: 'The only way for a woman, as for a man, to find herself as a person, is by creative work of her own. There is no other way. But a job, any job, is not the answer - in fact, it can be part of the trap. Women who do not look for jobs equal to their capacity, who do not let themselves develop the lifetime interests and goals which require serious education and training... are walking, almost as surely as the ones who stay inside the housewife trap, to a nonexistent future.... If a job is to be the way out of the trap for a woman, it must be a job that she can take seriously as part of a life plan, work in which she can grow as part of society.'"

Finished with their meals, Cosette ordered a tiramisu and a warm chocolate cake with pistachio gelato to share, as well as glasses of Amaretto. Once the dessert and liqueur were served, Yvette continued with her talk, "The next important second-wave feminist was Germaine Greer, who offered her thoughts on feminism in the 1970 bestseller, *The Female Eunuch*. She emphasizes in the 'Summary' of her book the importance of the sexual revolution for the liberation of women: 'Revolution ought to entail the correction of some of the false perspectives which our assumptions about womanhood, sex, love and society have combined to create. Tentatively it gestures towards the re-deployment of energy, no longer to be used in repression, but in desire, movement and creation. Sex must be rescued from the traffic between powerful and powerless, masterful and mastered, sexual and neutral, to become a form of communication between potent, gentle, tender people...'

"In the book's final section, 'Revolution', Greer delivers a message on the struggle for women's liberation: 'The surest guide to the correctness of the path that women take is "joy in the struggle." Revolution is the festival of the oppressed. For a long time there may be no perceptible reward for women other than their new sense of purpose and integrity. Joy does not mean riotous glee, but it does mean the purposive employment of energy in a self-chosen enterprise. It does mean pride and confidence. It does mean communication and cooperation with others based on delight in their company and your own.'"

With a wonderful dinner and conversation at an end, Cosette, Yvette and Sam left Original Joe's and walked down Union to Columbus. None of them looked over to where the killing occurred in Washington Square the night before last, for they all preferred to be free of the case, at least until the next day. Once on Columbus, they turned north for the walk to Cosette's apartment. Arm in arm, with Sam in the middle and quickly in a Zen-like state, Yvette started singing Cosette's favorite girlhood song, *I Am Woman*, with Cosette joining in on the chorus.

Once at Cosette's apartment, Yvette went inside while Cosette and Sam said goodnight at the front entrance, during which Sam said, "Please don't ever put me through that song again."

Cosette laughed and replied, "I promise, Sam, for I know it must have been excruciating for you."

"You have no idea, Cosette," Sam added. "If the MLB or NFL ever learns that I'm tied to that song, I'll get banned from all Giants' and 49ers' games... probably for life."

Laughing, Cosette kissed him gently on the cheek, then turned and went into her apartment.

Sam walked back to Columbus, hailed a cab and headed back to his apartment. And along the way he couldn't get the thought of that kiss out of his mind, nor the melody and lyrics to the Nat King Cole classic, *Almost Like Being in Love*.

Fisherman's Wharf and Nob Hill

A Questionable Suicide off the Golden Gate

Sam was back to his usual schedule and daily rituals the next morning: dressed and caffeinated in the apartment, breakfasted and caffeinated at the Golden Coffee while not pistol-whipping any of the patrons for their morning choices, and delivered to work along the same route to the office. Once at his desk, he turned the page of his "Private Investigator Word of the Day Calendar." That day's recommended term was "big sleep," as in dead. As he pondered the phrase, Sam thought back to an investigation conducted by his other dad, Philip Marlowe. His LA dad had named that one "The Case of the Big Sleep."

The problem with that case was that he let a drinking buddy, Raymond Chandler, write it up in 1939 for him as a favor. But due to his friend's propensity to remain drunk most of the time, the story that made it into print had many factual errors and left out several important events. As a consequence, most of the screenplay for the Bogey movie scripted by William Faulkner, who also wasn't afraid of a drink, was never checked with his dad as to what happened and what didn't happen. Anyway, Sam always remembered his dad's version of the investigation.

Just then the phone rang and Sam heard Tom's voice on the other end, "Sam, better get down to Crissy Field. Another girl washed up on the beach just east of Torpedo Wharf sometime during the night."

"Thanks, Tom," Sam replied, "I'll be right down. Can you see if there are any track marks on the girl's arms for me?"

Sam closed his office, left the building, and caught a cab down to Crissy Field, a former U.S. Army airfield, now part of the Golden Gate National Recreation Area. After taking over management in 1994, the National Park Service cleaned up the locale and in 2001 opened the Crissy Field Center, an environmental education complex.

Crissy Field offers beaches and dunes, tidal wetlands and trails, and a promenade popular with walkers and bikers alike.

Once down on the beach by the wharf, Sam saw Tom and motioned for him to come over. Tom walked over and said, "Sam, that young girl's body is pretty beaten up, but I'd lay odds that it's the twin of the one the other day at the Sutro Baths, track marks and all. And get this, Sam, the Lieutenant ordered us to report her as a suicide off the bridge."

"So she copped the big sleep," Sam said. "By the way, you ever heard of a club owner by the name of Gutt?"

"Yeh, Sam, he's connected with one of the strip joints up on Broadway," Tom answered. "I don't know which one though, but I can look into it for you."

"Do that, will you, Tom, and thanks again," Sam replied as he walked off to the promenade.

Once on the walkway, Sam phoned Cosette, "A young girl washed up down by Crissy Field sometime last night. My friend Tom identified her as the other twin. As you can imagine, like her sister, she copped the big sleep. I want you and Yvette to meet me at the Buena Vista Cafe, in say, an hour."

Before heading back to the Promenade for the walk to the Buena Vista, Sam looked across San Francisco Bay to the Golden Gate Bridge, more appropriately called the "Rusty Red Bridge." He always reminded himself that since its opening in 1937, this overly-touted erection had never been golden in color, because it had never been painted anything but rusty red. Why the City of San Francisco persisted in perpetuating the notion concerning its true color was always a source of dismay to him. Sam then turned towards the north to view the other world renowned sight in the Bay, that being Alcatraz, a place that was once an abode to the sorts of hardened criminals that today call the White House and Congress home.

Back on the Golden Gate Promenade, Sam walked east and noticed the tail from the day before, who was once again shadowing him. This time though, he was dressed in a Hawaiian shirt, shades and a Dodgers' cap. To see if he'd learned anything from his learning moment at the Hi Dive, Sam circled around the visitor's center and then continued along the promenade, stopping occasionally. Sure enough, the shadow matched his every step. Then he walked across the little bridge near the estuary and into the unlit bathroom at E Beach.

When the mug entered, Sam used a disposable instamatic camera that he always carried so as to blind him momentarily. He next threw his tail against a wall, reached for his gun with his left hand, and then pistol-whipped him on the right side of the man's skull. Like the day before, the tail went down, though now with a matching gash on the other side of his head. Sam then explained, "You know, buddy, you gave me no choice. Now who sent you to shadow me? Was it Gutt?"

Seeing that the man was only semi-conscious, Sam offered him another learning moment. "Now, William," he began, "let's review your steps from earlier. Wearing a Hawaiian shirt might be a good choice of attire in Los Angeles, but not in San Francisco, except maybe in The Castro. And the shades, possibly, except for the fact that it's a typical foggy summer day along the bay. Finally, the Dodgers cap is a definite no-no if you want to fit in in Giants' country."

"As regards tailing someone in a circle," Sam continued, "that's a dead giveaway. And when I stopped occasionally along the promenade, you should have passed me by, for you never let your mark approach you."

As the man began to pass out, Sam gave him a final word of encouragement, "But at least you made a good effort, keep up the fine work, William. And I'm glad to see you didn't bring your bean-shooter with you today. Unfortunately for you, I brought mine." And with that said, the shadow passed out.

An Irish Coffee at Fisherman's Wharf

Sam continued east along the promenade to the Yacht Harbor, then along Marina Boulevard past Marina Green. He next walked up the hill to the Great Meadow and followed the trail around Fort

Mason to Aquatic Park. After walking around the perimeter of the park, he cut across Victoria Park to the Buena Vista Cafe at 2765 Hyde Street, across from the Powell-Hyde cable car terminus. Since 1952, the Buena Vista has been famed in town and beyond for its superb Irish coffee.

When Sam arrived, Cosette and Yvette, as well as Karette, who was soon introduced to him, were already at a table enjoying their Irish coffees. When the waitress arrived, Sam ordered a straight coffee and a shot of Irish whiskey on the side. The waitress looked at him suspiciously, for heaven help the misguided soul who doesn't order an Irish coffee when in the Buena Vista. The four next ordered lunches, after which, Sam asked, "So what did you manage to find out this morning."

"Well, Sam," Cosette began, "Karette dropped by the apartment this morning and introduced the two of us to the online site for the Bay Area Sex Worker Advocacy Network, commonly known as BAYSWAN. It's a non-profit organization that attempts to improve working conditions, increase salaries and benefits, and eliminate discrimination for individuals working in legal and illegal aspects of the adult entertainment industry. The association also provides information to social services, policy reformers, media outlets and politicians. These may include the San Francisco Task Force on Prostitution, the Commission on the Status of Women, and any other local law enforcement agencies dealing with sex workers.

"From the beginning, BAYSWAN's purpose was to create a network of social service organizations, service providers, and community members to advocate on behalf of sex workers, massage parlor employees, escort services, exotic dancers, and other sex industry workers to protect their civil and workplace rights. BAYSWAN also works to improve communication between sex industry workers and government agencies, social service providers and other organizations."

Karette then interjected, "In 1996 it was BAYSWAN that provided support to the workers at the Lusty Lady Theatre in their efforts with the Exotic Dancers Alliance to unionize club workers. With the help of the Service Employees International Union, Local 790, in 1997 the Lusty Lady employees voted to form the Exotic Dancers Union, the first sex workers' organization of its kind, and to move towards establishing the club as a worker-owned cooperative.

"This was important for a number of reasons, not the least of which was that many clubs classified its dancers as 'independent contractors', charging its workers 'stage fees' or 'booking fees'. As you may or may not know, 'independent contractors' aren't covered by the laws that guarantee workers with 'employee status' the right to unionize. Needless to say, the club owners, almost all men, tried to prevent the unionization of workers, with any attempt to create closed shop working conditions met with immediate firings."

"We also visited another important website this morning," Cosette continued. "The Commission on the Status of Women is a branch of the City and County of San Francisco whose purpose is to ensure women and girls equal economic, social, political, and educational opportunities throughout the city. It was established by the San Francisco Board of Supervisors in 1975, and in 1994 the voters approved the creation of the City Department on the Status of Women."

At that point Sam faded out of the conversation and realized that he hadn't been to the Buena Vista in at least a year, mainly because his investigations seldom took him to Fisherman's Wharf. He also realized that one of these days he needed to get down to the Wharf to enjoy his usual martini in the Gold Dust Lounge at 165 Jefferson Street. The original Gold Dust opened on Powell Street, just around the corner from Lefty O'Doul's, in 1966. It remained at that location until a few years back, when it moved itself lock, stock and barrel to its new location in Fisherman's Wharf.

In the old days, Sam spent many memorable evenings in the Gold Dust. It was especially memorable when he ran into Herb Caen enjoying his usual Vitamin V: vodka served in a wine glass over ice, with a splash of soda and an orange wedge garnish. The last time Sam saw his fellow lounge-mate was in 1997, the year that San Francisco's most popular journalist died after almost sixty years as the "voice and conscience" of the city. He was asked by the then mayor to look into why this man became so important to the town, and he called the investigation, "The Case of the Wit and Wisdom of Herb Caen":

Born in Sacramento in 1916, after high school Herbert Eugene "Herb" Caen covered sports for *The Sacramento Union*. He joined the staff of the *San Francisco Chronicle* in 1936 writing a radio column, but two years later switched to a daily column on the city under the heading "It's News to Me." Caen wrote non-stop for the *Chronicle* - except for a four-year stint in the Air Force during World War II and an eight-year stint with the *San Francisco Examiner* from 1950-1958 - about local happenings and city gossip, offering curious anecdotes and interesting sketches.

Caen's most famous collection of essays, *Baghdad by the Bay*, a term that he coined to reflect the city's diversity, was published in 1949. That compilation was followed over the years by *Baghdad: 1951, Don't Call It Frisco, Herb Caen's Guide to San Francisco, Only in San Francisco*, and others. In 1996 he received a special Pulitzer Prize for "extraordinary and continuing contribution as a voice and conscience of his city." He continued to write until his death in 1997, and in leaving the city he also left behind his many years of wit and wisdom: "I hope I go to Heaven, and when I do, I'm going to do what every San Franciscan does when he gets there. He looks around and says, 'It ain't bad, but it ain't San Francisco.'"

With lunch now over, the four of them decided to take the Powell-Hyde cable car to the top of California. Andrew Hallidie engineered the first cable car line in 1873, with eight lines running by 1912. Only three lines remain today: the Powell-Mason, the Powell-Hyde, and the California. The Cable Car Barn and Powerhouse at 1201 Mason Street remains the place to visit for those with an interest in the engineering aspects and the fascinating history of the San Francisco cable car system. And just as the car took off, everyone onboard started singing *The Trolley Song.*

A Curious Dream on Nob Hill

At the top of California, the four of them jumped off, while the rest of the riders remained onboard singing that all-time classic. They walked west on California, past The Fairmont Hotel and The Huntington Hotel, and further along to Huntington Park atop Nob Hill. They sat down at a couple of benches that faced the fountain and Grace Cathedral. As they relaxed and enjoyed the warm summer sun and the light bay breeze, a woman walked by leading a black Maltese, saying as she went: "Come along, Falcon!" Sam thought: "Strange, very strange."

As the ladies talked, in his mind Sam reviewed what he knew about the case. He knew that the club where the twin girls were being prostituted was owned by a guy named Gutt, but he didn't know which club. He'd no idea who at City Hall was visiting the girls, nor why the cops had been ordered not to pursue the case, though he had his suspicions. And he hadn't a clue as to who the killer was, nor any idea as to his whereabouts. In other words, he'd no critical information at all for wrapping up the investigation. So, frustrated and exhausted, Sam closed his eyes and fell into a deep sleep.

While Sam slept, Yvette asked Cosette and Karette the fundamental question for today's feminists, "Why has the exploitation of women continued after all the strides that feminists have made in Western societies over the years? First-wave feminists in America and Europe were united in their goals of women's voting and property rights, these being the central issues of their generation. Similarly, the generation of the second-wave feminists offered their own shared goals and areas of concern within the feminist movement, with only slight differences between the liberal agenda in America and the socialist agenda in Europe. However, does a united women's front still exist in the feminist movement today? And if not, how will that affect the liberation of women today and in the future?

"To address those essential questions, let's review what has occurred in the last four decades. Beginning with Germaine Greer, a period of twenty years elapsed before the ushering in of what's called 'third-wave feminism' in the early Nineties. Although many historians of feminism view the American second-wave as ending in the early Eighties, actually, a breakdown in a united feminist agenda could already be seen in the latter Seventies. In part, this loss of momentum was brought on by the belief that everything had been accomplished within the feminist framework. Also, there were the internal disputes of the Feminist Sex Wars, mainly over issues such as sexuality and pornography. Along with this, there was a backlash to feminism by the underlying patriarchal elements of American society, which throughout the history of the nation had always been politically conservative and primarily religious-based.

"However, in the Autumn 1981 edition of the journal *Signs*, a Bulgarian-French feminist Julia Kristeva wrote an essay, 'Women's Time', in which she commented on the changes that were occurring in the feminist movement. In that article Kristeva identified the various waves in feminism, starting with what she called the 'first generation'. First-wave feminism's project was inclusion in the 'social contract', with a woman now the equal of a man and a view that there was essentially only one sex, that being Man. Kristeva then proceeded to identify the 'second generation' of feminism. Second-wave feminism's project was inclusion in the 'gender contract', with a woman now different from a man and the view that there are two sexes, Woman and Man.

"Concluding the essay, Kristeva offered her belief that a 'third generation' of feminism was emerging in society. Third-wave feminism's project would be inclusion in the 'existential contract', with a woman not only different from a man but also from other women, and the view that there may be more than two sexes. Kristeva ended her essay by pointing out the societal challenges that will accompany this emerging concept of individual difference.

"A decade later, in the early Nineties, the third-wave of feminism ushered in, as Kristeva predicted in her essay. Much of the intellectual aspects of the movement were attached to French Theory and Postmodernist thought that surfaced during the Sixties and Seventies in Europe, with those ideas then re-interpreted to suit the needs of American academics in the Eighties and Nineties. An excellent resource for understanding current trends in feminist thought is *Third Wave Feminism: A Critical Exploration*, edited by Stacy Gillis, Gillian Howie and Rebecca Munford, and published in 2007.

"Imelda Whelehan in the 'Foreword' of that collection of essays offered several points that differentiate third-wave from second-wave feminist thought. Third-wave feminists object to the doctrinaire positions of second-wave feminists and believe that they don't need leadership icons from a past generation. Instead, the Internet allows for small groups of women to discuss specific issues in their own ways, with feminist egalitarianism typical of all collectives. So there is no longer an essential school of feminist thought, but instead, all ideas are defined by the immediate needs of the individual woman or group of women.

"Needless to say, when women work together only within small groups, that limiting social connection poses a very real problem to forming a still much needed united feminist movement. Without a historical understanding of the sacrifices and contributions made by first-wave and second-wave feminists, there is no possibility that women may come to see themselves as members of a tradition that affects women everywhere and at all times.

"Also, given that third-wave feminists embrace popular culture and use it for their own purposes, this makes women completely dependent on that particular form of expression, with personal and confessional dialogue passing for feminist thought. And let us not forget that that popular technological culture is created mostly by men, with women easily used to further the ends of men, not women. Furthermore, keeping women divided works into a backlash agenda against feminism, allowing for the continued male domination of society.

"In the 'Introduction' of that book, the editors also offered some thoughts on the generational divide. Of course, all three waves of feminism are present in society today, but feminists are too divided along generational lines. However, these generational differences have replaced political differences to the detriment of women. In the 'Afterword' essay, 'Feminist Waves', Jane Spencer describes the incredible diversity of third-wave feminist groups: socialist feminists, utopia feminists, transgender feminists, racial feminists, Third World feminists, eco-feminists, as well as many others. Clearly, there is today a need for a global feminist strategy, though one undoubtedly based on pluralism."

While the three women talked about the issues confronting feminism, Sam was in a deep sleep, during which he experienced a curious dream concerning an unknown man:

He is a travel writer and an avid reader of French literature and poetry, as well as French history and philosophy. One night he meets a much younger and quite bewitching Parisian woman at a dinner party of a friend. They spend the evening in *tête-à-tête*, which reminds him of something the French academic Jacque Barzun said in 1959, now included as the epitaph of the 2002 collection, *A Jacques Barzun Reader*: "The finest achievement of human society and its rarest pleasure is Conversation." At the end of the night, he asks if he might get to know her better and she agrees to have a meal with him.

A few weeks later at dinner, he discovers that she's the most open and honest woman he ever met, and easily the most fascinating. After she tells him all about herself, he realizes that her story as a Parisian dancer is much more complicated than at first thought. He tells her that he would like to use her life journey in a travel book on Paris. At the end of the evening they agree to see each other more often and to correspond on a regular basis. They also agree that due to certain unstated circumstances in her life, they must commit to remaining good friends and nothing else.

Several weeks pass and he decides that he must also write about her in a detective story, one in which he tells the world about her fascinating life. In writing her journeys, he becomes aware that he's only ever written with his mind, never with his heart. He realizes that the passion he feels because of his relationship with her is now critically important to his writing, to his very creativity, to his very soul. And he finally understands the meaning of Sarah Vaughn's rendition of *I Could Write a Book*.

Over time he gets to know her better through a constant flow of missives, at dinners in secluded restaurants, and during rendezvous' in the city. They both come to enjoy everything about their little trysts: the sharing of food and wine, the reading of French novels and poetry, and the asking of life's questions never answered. At one of their meetings, he tells her that she inspired him to such an extent that he wrote her a poem, *The Beginning of Their Journey*:

Two wandering souls in search of a Muse
One through the celebration of the dance
The other through the pleasure of the word
Begin a sublime journey together

They met an unexpected wintry Eve
Over good food, fine wine, engaging talk
Then the words came forth to trouble his mind
She was proclaimed: *La Siren dans le mer*

He asked, "Who is this erotic creature?"
She, a vision of 'eternal beauty'
Sculpted Athena by the ancient Greeks
Painted Madonna by the Old Masters

But Botticelli immortalized her
One hand covering her untouched full breast
The other shielding virgin innocence
Captured for all time, *The Birth of Venus*

She asked, "Who is this peculiar creature?"
He, a writer with name and words unknown
Still, her interest took him by surprise
And he wished to bare her mystery

An exchange of thoughts passed from day to day
They tried to meet, with plans ever changing
Then one day all celestial stars aligned
With a rendezvous set in place and time

They dined that evening, with connection made
And with wine flowing, shared both thoughts and dreams
Then over time a budding friendship grew
With conversation shaping a vision

Together in hand they would tell a tale
Of life, of death, of joy, of woe, of love
Of three waves that break upon shifting shores
Such was the beginning of their journey

He eventually comes to understand that before they met, he
was a man asleep, a man in a coma, and that she was the
one who woke him from his eternal slumber. He also now
understands what Honoré de Balzac meant in his 1833 novel
Eugénie Grandet: "The spirit, like the body, must breathe to

live: it needs to take in love, from another soul, like oxygen, make it part of itself, and give it back, enriched. Without that wonderful process the heart dies: it suffers from lack of air and ceases to beat."

For some unknown reason, the more he sees her the more she challenges his long-held perceptions of women and of life. Through her close friendship, he realizes that he's always suffered from an inability to relate openly and honestly with a woman. In the course of time, she completely redefines him as a writer and as a man. And as the seasons quickly pass by, his affection for her increases and he can't imagine his life without her friendship.

One day he receives a call from her that she must see him immediately. She arrives at his door just as the night sky envelopes his apartment in darkness. After she comes in, they sit on the couch next to each other. She takes his hands in hers and puts her head on his shoulder. He places his arm around to embrace her and asks why she seems so sad. She explains to him that this is the last time they'll ever see each other, for she's leaving for Paris in the morning. She asks him not to ask why, but to just accept her personal circumstances without question. He brings out a sonnet he wrote for her and reads *The Yellow Rose*:

A poet strolled through a garden one day
Enjoying a flower each step of the way
He soon spied a rose begging him follow
Coming he found a wee shoot of yellow

The yellow rose begged him, "look upon me
Though only a bud, my soul soon you'll see"
And as he began to study her more
She blossomed forth joy to join with amour

His longing eyes watched, while heart filled with thirst
With full bloom he thought, the sun had just burst
Its glowing warmth filled his cold heart with bliss
He lowered his lips, love sealed with a kiss

He now spends his days in sonnet and prose
Loving forever the beautiful rose

After listening to the poem, she tells him that she has shared her thoughts and feelings with him more than she ever thought possible with a man. He agrees that he feels the same way and that he doesn't know what he'll do without having her to talk with any longer. She says that as they've shared all they possibly can with their minds and their hearts, there's only one way left in which to share themselves. She reaches her hands up to caress his face and draws his lips gently down to hers for their first kiss...

The next morning she's gone from his life and he wonders how he can continue to write, continue to be creative. Despite his constant questioning over the next few months, he can't explain to himself how meeting such a woman, a seemingly random event, could change his life so completely. He analyzes himself in vain to understand his new attitude in how he faces the world and how he confronts the writer's task.

Then one day while reading Jacques Barzun, he finds an answer to his many questions in the author's 2000 masterpiece, *From Dawn to Decadence*: "Is this a mystery or not? No answer seems conclusive if we ponder any important changes in ourselves... occasionally [caused] by an emotional shock. Again, when our minds undergo sudden, profound alterations - in opinion or belief, in love, or in what is called artistic inspiration - what is the ultimate cause? We see the results, but grasp the chain of reasoning at a link well below the hook from which it hangs."

Over time he learns to accept that life is full of essential questions for which there are no definitive answers, and that he must merely enjoy his new perceptions of the world. He also continues to write about two investigations, one set in San Francisco and one set in Paris, with both places surging with his memories of her. As the seasons once again quickly pass by, and with the books finally written, one morning he awakens to find a missive from her...

As the gals ended their discussion on third-wave feminism, Sam woke up to find Cosette, Yvette and Karette ready to take off. Cosette said to him, "I've got a performance tonight down at The Church in The Mission, but this afternoon Karette wants us to visit the Center for Sex and Culture where she now works. Since I'll probably be dressing for my performance, meet my mom and Karette in the bar about a quarter to eight. I'll get a guest pass for you and give it to mom."

Sam replied, "That works out great as I've got some work to do on the case, but I need to do it alone. I should have everything wrapped up by tonight." Once on the street, Sam put the three ladies in a cab to The Mission, while he took off on foot for his apartment.

The Tenderloin and The Fillmore

Celebrated Criminal Cases of America

Sam walked south down the hill along Taylor Street to Post and then turned west to his apartment. As he walked in the door, he got a call from Tom, "Sam, you've got to meet me in the Bourbon & Branch in The Tenderloin in an hour. I've got some important information for you."

"Thanks, Tom, I'll see you then," Sam replied. With some time to blow, he picked up his copy of Thomas S. Duke's *Celebrated Criminal Cases of America*. He'd been meaning to re-read his dad's favorite book from 1910 for some time, so he opened the pages to the preface: "This volume, which is the first history published of the celebrated criminal cases in America, includes the most important cases during the past eighty years. They have been collected after years of systematic investigation and verified with the assistance of police officials throughout America, without whose co-operation an authentic history would be impossible. The hundred and ten cases presented in this volume should prove interesting to the general reader because of the psychological and, in many cases, the historical interest which attaches to them."

Sam next looked over the contents the book, which was divided into three parts: San Francisco Cases, Celebrated Cases on Pacific Coast, and Celebrated Cases East of the Pacific Coast. He then thumbed through the pages until coming to the photographs showing the City Marshalls and Chiefs of San Francisco Police. Unbeknownst to most of the residents these days, many of the streets in San Francisco were named after those no-nonsense cops of no-nonsense times, an era now long since past. After that, Sam began reading the first chapter on San Francisco Cases, one titled "A History of the San Francisco Police Department."

After finishing the chapter, Sam turned the TV on to the Ra Ra Right channel, where a conservative presidential contender was outlining his proposals for transforming public education:

> During my administration public schools will be replaced by private faith-based institutions that teach students the way God intended them to be taught... good and hard. Once my agenda is in place, the Secretary of Conservative Education will outline to the nation the introduction of right and proper curriculum materials into every educational institution.

> The Secretary will point out that for too many years now the American people, as well as their loving and obedient children, have had to suffer the horror and repugnance of a li-ber-al education. By li-ber-al is meant a public education that spends far too much time in activities that seldom result in increased earning potential later in life and that also turn them away from the true American god, Midas. And the public, soon to be private and faith-based, primary school day will offer the following right and proper agenda:

> *Morning Religious Observance (8:00-8:30)*: This most important period of the school day begins with a moment of silence, a time during which non-Christians are politely asked to stand outside the room so as not to afflict the devout with their heathen thoughts. This moment of solitude is followed by a reading of the Ten Commandments, which is a document that's posted in at least one dozen conspicuous places in every classroom. Finally, and to encourage each student's dramatic abilities, a morality play of the Old School is rendered in front of the class. And though every teacher may select his or her class performances, all plays should emphasize Jesus' entrepreneurial spirit as the CEO of a private faith-based global corporation.

Morning Patriotic Observance (8:30-9:00): This second most important period of the day begins with the "Pledge of Allegiance," which now takes a new form: "I pledge allegiance to the sacred flag of the United States of America, and to the corporations for which it stands, one conglomerate, under the Christian God, with fewer taxes for some and fewer services for all." The new pledge is followed by the singing of the *National Anthem, God Bless America, My Country 'Tis of Thee* and the *Marine Corps Hymn*. The last part of the observance is a talk by the teacher on a subject of his or her choosing, though that lecture should always bring out the importance of never asking the government for assistance of any kind, except for assistance in opting out of public education.

American Mathematics Lesson (9:00-9:30): All lessons in mathematics emphasize the importance of one's personal financial affairs, with that fact driven home by the rewriting of arithmetic books so that all numbers are preceded by dollar signs. Suggested topics include: Paying for My Education without Government Assistance, Paying for My Healthcare without Government Assistance, and Paying for My Retirement without Government Assistance. And at the end of the lesson, students are offered government assistance to transfer to private faith-based educational institutions.

American Mathematics Testing (9:30-10:00): To emphasize the importance of competition in the proper running of American society, as well as to better prepare children for the dog-eat-dog competencies needed in the modern workplace, students are tested on a daily basis in certain core subjects. The results of these tests are printed in local, state and national papers so as to embarrass poorly performing schools and teachers into doing a better job. Also, teachers whose students perform exceptionally well are encouraged to leave the public school system in favor of teaching in private faith-based educational institutions.

Nutrition Break (10:00-10:15): To acquaint students with a fine snack traditionally enjoyed by the good people of the southern states and MLB players, chewing tobacco is the mainstay of the nutrition break. Unfortunately, the genteel and refined use of chaw has been in decline for a number of years now, which is a trend that has been particularly disturbing to the tobacco industry. Hopefully, with the necessary encouragement from primary school teachers, students can once again enjoy a wholesome and time-honored American tradition.

Morning Recess (10:15-10:30): Sports during recess should emphasize the importance of competition in all facets of American life, and any competition that does not result in a clear-cut winner is excised from the curriculum. However, since girls tend to outperform boys in lower age groups, the sexes never play games together until the upper grades, when the boys can at last physically dominate the girls. This practice guarantees that all boys retain a strong and virile competitive spirit, which is an important attribute that eventually translates into increased productivity in the workplace. In addition, this practice also guarantees that girls lose their interest in sports at an early age, and as well, it convinces them that happiness in life comes through applying makeup and encouraging the boys to do their very best.

Mid-Morning Religious Observance (10:30-11:00): After another moment of silence, there's a second reading of the Ten Commandments. Students then join together in singing a few heartwarming classics, such as *Jesus Loves Me*, *Onward Christian Soldiers*, and *Michael (not Mary) Row the Boat Ashore*. The teacher of course chastises students of non-Christian faiths until they sing along as well, for only in this way can heathens find the path to a right and proper heaven.

American English Lesson (11:00-11:30): English lessons are organized around only two books, those being Ayn Rand's *The Fountainhead* and Milton Friedman's *Capitalism and Freedom*. Student time is spent copying sections of these two important works, though better students are also encouraged to memorize selections for recital in front of their classmates. At the end of the lesson, students are once again offered government assistance to transfer to private faith-based educational institutions.

American English Testing (11:30-12:00): See American Mathematics Testing.

Lunch (12:00-12:30): Since studies show that school performance began to decline when ethnic foods entered the school lunch program, there will be a return to the time-honored American lunch favorites, namely, the hamburger and chips, the hot dog and chips, and spaghetti that doesn't smell like Mediterranean people. And to complete every wholesome lunchtime meal, dessert is another mouthful of good old chaw.

Afternoon Patriotic Observance (12:30-1:00): Play-acting is the cornerstone of this second patriotic observance of the day, with students encouraged to reenact popular and public-spirited activities. Examples of these dramas might include harassing disadvantaged women as they enter Planned Parenthood clinics, purchasing semi-automatic weapons at neighborhood gun shows, and chastising people who ask for any form of government assistance. At the end of the observance, students are once again offered government assistance to transfer to private faith-based educational institutions.

American Science Lesson (1:00-1:30): As is only right and proper, the emphasis during science class revolves around three major areas of concern. Firstly, the military science for carrying out Preemptory Strikes is clearly explained to students, with any peacenik objections dismissed outright as the preposterous notions of unpatriotic bleeding-heart li-ber-als. Secondly, Creationism and Intelligent Design are taught as the only true sciences of the world, while the Myth of Evolution is demonized as the evil work of godless heathens. Lastly, the importance of Man's creature comforts, ones that are provided to him by the benevolent work of unregulated global corporations, is pointed out, with any democratic and environmental concerns of the students dismissed as rubbish pandered by trouble-making one-world Socialists.

American Science Testing (1:30-2:00): See American Mathematics Testing.

Afternoon Recess: Because of a massive tax reduction given to the deserving wealthy, the afternoon recess is eliminated from the curriculum due to further cutbacks in public education.

American History Lesson (2:00-2:30): All history lessons emphasize the undisputed fact that America, and only America, created all that is right and proper in the world. This of course is most easily accomplished by having Hollywood scriptwriters continue rewriting much of world history, though now as scripts for children's lessons. Since antisocial children from dysfunctional families sometimes, through their history lessons, come to needlessly question the motives and actions of their well-meaning civic and business leaders, critical thinking of any sort is discouraged as being unpatriotic and un-American.

American History Lesson: No testing in American History is necessary, for all test questions have one and only one correct answer... the American one.

Afternoon Religious Observance (2:30-3:00): The last period of the school day is turned over to one long moment of silence, when students promise Jesus that they will never ask for government assistance of any kind. This is followed by a final reading of the Ten Commandments. And as before, at the end of the observance students are once again offered assistance to transfer to private faith-based educational institutions.

Once the program ended, Sam thought about how historians would one day write a second volume of *Celebrated Criminal Cases of America*. That much needed book would chronicle the nearly forty years of unjust, undemocratic, and perhaps unconstitutional crimes perpetrated against American public school children. It would outline in great detail the numerous attempts by most of the Republicans to privatize education, and by many of the Democrats to privatize and federalize education.

Sam also thought about the primary flaw of "Obamacore," at least as regards the teaching of mathematics. Given that most school teachers have only experienced the traditional approach in learning mathematics, many possess inadequate quantitative and statistical skills to implement a new and progressive approach. However, Sam had hope that somewhere in America an educational investigator would offer a possible solution to that widespread and critical problem.

A Speak Easy in The Tenderloin

At a quarter to five, Sam turned the TV off and left his apartment. He walked east on Post to Jones, then south to the Bourbon & Branch at 501 Jones Street in The Tenderloin. The Twenties-style speakeasy is a throwback to Prohibition times and it sits on the actual location of a bar that operated illegally from 1921 to 1933. The name of the bar, "Bourbon & Branch," comes from a Prohibition-era request for bourbon and clean water. And the term "speakeasy" was the quiet manner in which a patron was supposed to order his booze, namely, to "speak easy."

As Sam sipped at his bourbon on the rocks, he thought back to an investigation he conducted some years before. That one involved a fellow imbiber of bourbon and he named it "The Case of the Extraordinary Emperor":

Around 1815, the British Isles sent forth into the world a man by the name of Joshua A. Norton. He arrived in San Francisco in 1849, carrying with him an agreeable fortune. Once in the city, Norton convinced his agreeable fortune to become even more agreeable, and to the tune of a quarter million dollars. But in 1854 he got to figuring and came up with what he thought was a sure fire plan to double or even triple his agreeable fortune.

Joshua Norton then went about his plan of cornering the rice market, though unfortunately, he accidentally missed out on a couple of the corners. So now completely broke, he left the city and didn't return for three years. Now it's at this point that the story evolves from the ordinary to the extraordinary, and in doing so it becomes a fine tale of how you can't keep a majestic man down.

Upon his return to San Francisco in 1857, Joshua Norton triumphantly proclaimed himself: "Emperor of California."

But believing that the title might not be constitutional, he soon upped his station in life by declaring himself: "Norton I, Emperor of the United States and Protector of Mexico." So with full recognition of the obliging folks of San Francisco, the Emperor was soon proudly sauntering down city streets bowing magnanimously to his subjects and spending his days occupied in affairs of state.

The Emperor issued proclamations that were published in city newspapers, and as well, he printed his own currency that was accepted by many businesses. In addition, he ensured the observance of city ordinances, levied small taxes on local businesses, and fined anyone that referred to the city as "Frisco." The Emperor even went so far as to send off dispatches to officials in other American cities, as well as to Heads of State in the rest of the world. And prophetically, he ordered the construction of two bridges, one across the Golden Gate and another one over to Oakland.

The Emperor also dressed every bit the Emperor, for he attired himself in a brass-buttoned army uniform with huge epaulettes and adorned his head with a plumed hat, with those dignified articles thoughtfully provided to him by the San Francisco Board of Supervisors. And wherever he went, the Emperor was accompanied by his two most loyal subjects, Bummer and Lazarus, a couple of publicly-owned canines.

However, those two beasts were by no means equal subjects of the Emperor, for Lazarus was Bummer's "obsequious vassal" after having been rescued by the other cur during a street-fight one day. On the other hand, Bummer was famous for his heroic exploits along Montgomery Street, and he was forever deserving of great praise. In fact so much so that when Bummer thrust off the mortal coil of life, Mark Twain wrote in the November 11, 1865, edition of *The Californian* that "he died full of years, and honor, and disease, and fleas." And when the Emperor finally died in January of 1880, ten thousand San Franciscans filed past his casket to hail and toast him.

After Sam ordered his second bourbon, Tom walked in the door of the speakeasy. He went to the bar and ordered bourbon on the rocks for himself, and then sat down next to his longtime friend. Sam asked, "So, Tom, what do you have for me?"

"Well, Sam, I've got a load of information for you," Tom replied, "but you're not going to like any of it. First off, this guy Gutt owns the most exclusive club on Broadway. I mean, you've got to have plenty of money and connections just to get a foot in the door. Here's the name of the place." Tom pushed a card over to Sam and then continued, "But that's not all, Sam. Word on the street is that there's a contract out on you. Gutt's also aiming at that gal friend of yours if he can't get at you first. The both of you are in big danger. And believe me when I say, Central won't do a damn thing to protect you."

"That's good to know, Tom." Sam responded. "Neither Cosette nor I want to cop the big sleep. Any word on who might be the hit man for this little operation?"

"No idea about that, Sam," Tom answered, "but I do know that Sammy down in The Fillmore occasionally fills in for the regular piano player at Gutt's club."

"I'll head down to The Fillmore next and see if he's playing tonight," Sam said. "By the way, Tom, I thought the Lieutenant ordered you to stay clear of me."

"He did, Sam, but it doesn't matter anymore," Tom replied. "My application for an early retirement came through yesterday. I'll be out of Central tomorrow and I won't be looking back with any tears in my eyes."

"I'll miss you, Tom," Sam said to his long-time friend. "You've always done me right and I owe you more than one favor."

"Same to you, Sam," Tom agreed, "and here's how you can pay me back. I want you to watch your back on this one. I've never seen

City Hall so hell bent on burying a case in all my years on the force. I don't know what it's all about, but this one goes to the very top of the mayor's office."

"Thanks for the head's up, Tom," Sam replied. "Say, how about we meet for lunch tomorrow at John's Grill, maybe around two o'clock to miss the lunch crowd."

"Sounds good, Sam, tomorrow at two," Tom said as he got up. "It'll be just like the old days before this town got so damn complicated."

After Tom left the bar, Sam finished his bourbon. He then left the saloon and flagged down a cab that took him to The Fillmore to find Sammy.

A Jazz Session in The Fillmore

Within ten minutes, Sam was in The Fillmore at the Sheba Piano Lounge at 1419 Fillmore Street. The two blocks on Fillmore south of Geary are now the center for a revitalized city jazz scene, with Yoshi's San Francisco across from the lounge at 1300 Fillmore Street. The Fillmore, once known as "Harlem of the West," was a national center for jazz during the Forties and Fifties. Featuring several music venues in those days, the district was honored by most of the leading jazz luminaries: Louis Armstrong, John Coltrane, Ella Fitzgerald, Billie Holiday and Charlie Parker, to name but a few. And on the first weekend of July these days, The Fillmore also offers the Fillmore Street Jazz Festival, featuring local area talent on three stages that spread from Eddy Street to Geary and then north to Jackson Street.

As Sam walked in the door of the lounge, he was pleased to find Sammy at the piano. As usual, Sam said what he always said to Sammy, "You know what I want to hear. You played it for her, you can play it for me. If she can stand it, I can. Play it." Sammy laughed, and then tickled the ivories and sang the classic melody *As Time Goes By*.

While Sammy played and sang, Sam went to the bar and ordered his usual martini. When Sammy finished, Sam motioned for him to come to the bar. The piano player joined him and ordered a scotch on the rocks. Then Sam asked, "I need some help, Sammy. I heard you sometimes fill in for the regular piano player at Gutt's club on Broadway. Is that right?"

"You've got that right, Sam," Sammy answered hesitantly. "Why do you want to know?"

"Well, Sammy," Sam continued, "you've heard about the killing of that woman the other night at Washington Square and the girl that washed up onshore the other day at the Sutro Baths. Now you probably haven't heard that another young girl, the twin of the first, washed up along the Bay last night. Well, the cops are saying there's no connection between any of those three gals that copped the big sleep. I think there's a cover-up in the works and I want to damn well know why."

"Look, Sam, I shouldn't be telling you this," Sammy replied, "for if I get connected to any of this, I'm a dead man. I was working in Gutt's club the night the woman was killed in the Square. I saw her leave with the twins by the back door near the piano. I then saw one of Gutt's goons take off after them and heard the tires of a car screech outside the club."

Sam thought: "That explains why the missing homeless guy reported seeing a man shoot the woman and make off with the girls."

Sam then asked, "Do you know what the girls were doing in the club?"

"Look, Sam, this is only a rumor," Sammy answered, "but word around the club was that they were being used as personal prostitutes by some city official high up in the mayor's office. Being near the back door, I saw him show up on a couple of occasions."

Sam then asked, "Do you know who he is, Sammy?"

Sammy hesitated for a moment and so Sam said to him, "I don't like to say this, my friend, but you owe me a big favor."

"I know I do, Sam," Sammy responded, "but no one else must know what I'm going to tell you, otherwise I'll play dumb. You know the current mayor is being termed out at the next election. Well, this guy in the club is the hand-picked candidate to be the next Mayor of San Francisco."

"Thanks, Sammy, you've just put most of the pieces of the puzzle together for me," Sam replied.

Sam next thought: "That explains why the heat was on Central to report the killings as separate incidents. It also explains why there's a contract out on Cosette and me."

Sam then asked, "Now, any idea who the hit man might be that wants to offer me and a gal friend of mine the big sleep."

"Gutt only uses one goon that I know of," Sammy answered. "If there's a contract out on you, it'll be the same guy doing the job, the same guy that probably did in the woman and the twins. His name's Joe and he's a dead ringer for Peter Lorre. He's a nasty piece of work, Sam."

"Other than the club, do you have any idea where this guy can be found?" Sam questioned.

"The only place I ever saw him outside the club was in a Chinatown apartment that I've played several private gigs at," Sammy replied. "Most nights Joe gets there around eight o'clock for the usual party around nine. Those parties are attended by cops way up in the department and a few dancers from the bar. And, Sam, the girls don't just dance, if you know what I mean. The place is located on the northwest corner of Broadway and Stockton Street. It's the third-floor corner apartment with the boarded up windows."

"And what's this Gutt look like, Sammy?" Sam asked.

"He's a fat guy and looks a lot like Sydney Greenstreet," Sammy answered.

"Thanks, Sammy, you've been a great help to me," Sam said. "I owe you one big time."

Sammy returned to his piano and said to Sam as he passed by on his way out, "By the way, Sam, who's the gal friend you mentioned. It's not that stunner from a year or so back that you used to bring in here? I liked her, everyone in the place did. Anyway, take care and here's a song for the two of you." Sam smiled as he left the bar to another classic melody, this one, *It Had to Be You.*

The Mission and The Castro

A Beautiful Beat in The Mission

After leaving the piano lounge, Sam caught a cab to The Mission and The Church. Yvette and Karette were in the bar when he arrived around a quarter to eight, with Cosette changing backstage for her performance. Sam ordered himself his usual martini and then said, "Yvette, I don't want you to worry, but you and Cosette are going to spend the night at my place. After this afternoon, I've put most of the pieces of the investigation together and should wrap up the case tomorrow. However, early in the morning I want you to head back to your place in the wine country. This is just to be on the safe side. And don't worry about Cosette. I have another plan for her."

At a few minutes before eight o'clock, Yvette, Karette and Sam entered the music hall. The entertainment that night was to be three local acts, each performing for almost an hour. The first performance for the evening was Cosette and her partner, a Beat by the name of Kool Kat. When they came onstage, Sam was reminded of how sexy Cosette was in her performance outfits. That night she wore an all black ensemble: a loose-fitting blouse, skin-tight dance pants, and dancer's shoes. Her partner, Kool Kat, was also attired in all black: dress shirt and slacks, a spiffy pair of loafers, a Fifties-style fedora, and a tie with the colorful image of a tenor saxophone. Sam had never liked this Kool Kat, for the guy clearly had a thing for Cosette.

The presenter came to the microphone and announced the first act, "The Beatific Beats," and then the stage lights went out momentarily. As they came back on, Cosette sat on a high bar stool, while Kool Kat lounged in a comfortable chair with a huge book on his lap. He then told the audience, "I hope you Kats and Kits dig this evening. Every night my Kitten enjoys dancin' and singin' before she puts her little paws over her little kitty eyes and heads to Dreamsville. And to help her wind down from her very frenzied day, I read a story or two from 'Bedtime for Beats'. The first tale I'll tell her tonight is called, 'Tribute to Bop'."

At that point in the performance, the music began with Miles Davis' *Blue in Green*. And while Cosette performed her slow jazz dance, Kool Kat read her a beatific bedtime story:

One day a Bird hatched in a Kansas City nest
And as he learned to fly high
All the hipster birds taught him
To wing most sweet... like an upstart eagle

He soared first with the Big Band birds
Floating above the feathered flock
First in the Windy City
Then in... the Big Apple

And while diggin' the beat on Fifty-Second Street
A thing most unexpected occurred
When a sound was born unto the world
A reverberation to the ears... known as Bop

On one atmospheric night
Bird flew to a place no flyin' eagle ever flew before
And once there
He met... a Dizzy bird

That fellow feathered friend flew out of Carolina South
And just like Bird
Dizz first learned to fly with the Big Band birds
In Philly... and while wingin' on the other side of the pond

And also like Bird
He eventually came to roost on that famed street
And in that famed Bird-land

With other birds knowing not what to make... of these two
soaring eagles

The one blowin' his alto
And the other trumpetin' his horn
The one leadin' the way
And the other organizin' that way for other birds to follow...
intensely

All the young eaglets were soon emulatin' the Bopsters
With sounds unique unto them
Forever blowin' new thoughts into the warm still night
Of a world that is now... but a distant memory

Then all across that vast and untamed wilderness
That is America
The new and glorious sound took shape
On the wings... of the young flyers

One of those jazzlin's was the eaglet Miles
Delivered out of St. Louis
And his name was most hip
For he was soon... miles ahead

Though first blowin' with Bird's nest of five
Miles could never stop flyin' higher
And he soon went to school in the land of the Cool
Leading Bop onto another cloud floating aloft... amongst the
airy heights

Like Icarus with his feathers and wax
Miles flew too near the sun and crashed back to earth
But out of the ashes there emerged a new Phoenix
One who flew in the heavens higher than any eagle... ever
flew before

And after encouraging others to fly higher with him
Miles was soon quintetin'
And sextetin' the greatest Bop
That had ever been heard... in the world of jazzlin's

So whether those birds were cookin' or relaxin'
Workin' or steamin'
The resonance was forever kind of blue
With a new sound called... Modality

One of those kind of blue men was a bird
By the name of Trane
And he flew out of Carolina North
Eventually finding in Philly... that his sax was his only ax

The Dizzy bird was the first to take him under his wing
Though after he learned to fly high
The Trane choo-chooed his way to Miles' nest
For all that... quintetin' and sextetin'

But eventually this bird had to fly aloft alone
And whether he sang soprano or tenor
This Sax Man made the sweetest and most melancholic of
sounds
For any Kat who ever cared to listen... intensely

In Sixty-Five the Trane man was stopped in his tracks
Just as Bird had been ten years earlier
Miles and Dizz flew almost thirty years more
Forever flyin' high with sounds most clear... and most free

And if the world ever ends
Today or tomorrow or a million years from now
The lyrical thoughts of those four soaring eagles
Will deliver a message eternally... that it was not all in vain

With the first melody and Beat verse ended, Cosette returned to her chair. Then, Anita O'Day's version of *You're the Top* began to play, with Cosette dancing to the rhythm. And after a brief interlude, and with Cosette still dancing, Anita O'Day sang her very cool lyrics to the song.

When the second number ended, Cosette sat back on her stool, now shrouded in darkness, while Kool Kat turned to a new page in his bedtime book. He then said, "Another dance my Kitten enjoys is one I call 'Pygmalion's Appeal'. Sometimes she likes to hide from me by remaining ever so still. To find her, I first read a poem by the French Surrealist Paul Verlaine, one titled *My recurring dream.*"

While Kool Kat read the poem, a stage light grew slowly brighter over Cosette, who was now in a statuesque pose. And once the poem ended, Kool Kat read the prelude to *Oh, Lady be Good*, though with a few changes to the lyrics. Then, with Barney Kessel and Herb Ellis on guitars, the music to the main theme started with Cosette dancing slowly at first, though with a pace increasing throughout the song. While she danced, Kool Kat snapped his fingers, song-spoke the words, and occasionally offered some scat.

With the third number over, Cosette rested on her stool, which was once again shrouded in darkness. Kool Kat then turned to a new page in his book and said, "While my Kitten takes five, I often entertain her by reciting a few lines from 'The Bard of Avon', as interpreted by His Royal Hipness, Lord Buckley. So tonight I think you'll dig 'Marc Antony's Funeral Oration', Act 3, Scene 2, from *Julius Caesar.* When the introduction ended, Kool Kat stopped momentarily in his talk, looked about the hall in a condescendingly English manner, and then began his Beat version of the oration.

With the oration over, Kool Kat announced to the audience, "The Beatific Beats would like to make a request of all of you tonight. In the bar is a petition that will be sent to Congress to designate July 17 as National Scat Day. The purpose of this day will be to ask all American citizens and residents to refrain from using their normal language, and to instead speak to each other in the language of Scatese. For example, when two friends meet each other on the street on that day, instead of each saying, 'Hey, good to see you', each will say something like, 'Bebop do rebop' or 'Daba do weeee'.

"Now, for those in the audience that may not be fluent in Scat, Kool Kat's going to offer you a lesson tonight. Just then, the sounds of Clifford Brown's classic *Joy Spring* filled the auditorium, with Kool Kat scatting to the melody. He then stopped the music and asked everyone in attendance to join in a little jazz improvisation. And with *Joy Spring* once again filling the hall, the audience enjoyed its first lesson in the language of Scatese.

When the scat session ended, the stage light over Kool Kat went off and the one over Cosette went on. She started slowly dancing to the French song *Le Mer*, sung by Juliette Gréco. When the French version of the song ended, the light over Cosette went off and the one over Kool Kat went on as he recited a sea-faring poem, *The Storm-Tossed Sea*:

A schooner makes her steady way
Upon a storm-tossed sea
Her search for dreamt of gentle bay
A longed for home to be

Onboard, the ever-faithful crew
Work hand-in-hand on sail
To keep the ship on compass true
'Til sight of home they hail

And though at times direction lost
When winds blow where unknown
The crew forever bears the cost
Their hearts sing in one tone

So through the ebb and flow of time
The ship sails bravely on
The captain longs for Love sublime
With Her 'til last breathe gone

The poem at an end, the lights came on over Cosette, who fast danced to Bobby Darin's rendition of *Beyond the Sea*, with Kool Kat finger-poppin' to the beat. During the interlude of the song, Kool Kat got up and danced with Cosette. And as the last verse began, Kool Kat returned to his chair, while Cosette continued to dance slower and slower to the end of the tune.

Cosette next slowly moved her stool near Kool Kat, who watched her intently as Dorothy Dandridge sang *That's All*. At the end of the song, he said to the audience, "Sometimes my Kitten wants to go outside and play as her night draws to a close. So to dissuade her from her kittinish intentions, I have her join me in the song *Baby It's Cold Outside*."

With the song at an end, Cosette next moved her stool to the back of Kool Kat's chair, with the audience listening now to Wes Montgomery's version of *I've Grown Accustomed to Her Face*. She then kneeled next to Kool Kat, who spoke the lyrics while staring in her eyes.

The performance almost at an end, Kool Kat said to the audience, "It's time for my Kitten to head to Dreamsville. And she knows it's time when she hears her final song, Antonio Carlos Jobim's *Estrada do Sol*." As the melody played, Cosette got up danced slower and slower until she ended up in Kool Kat's lap with her head against his chest. With the performance now over, The Beatific Beats stood up, bowed to the audience, and left the stage.

A Third Wave in The Castro

After changing, Cosette found Yvette, Karette and Sam in the bar and they decided to head to The Castro for a drink. The four of them first walked up Valencia to 19th Street, then west through Delores Park to Castro Street.

On the way over, Sam told Cosette, "You and Yvette are going to spend the night at my place. I'll explain everything later, but it's nothing to worry about. By tomorrow our investigation will be over."

Continuing on, they strolled two blocks north to 401 Castro Street and Market, location of Twin Peaks Tavern, known as the "Gateway to the Castro." The panoramic windows of the bar offered views of the hustle and bustle that is The Castro, not only for gays and lesbians, but also for those who just want to observe an alternative slice of life in a welcoming bar. After the three luckily found a window table, Sam went to the bar for three whiskeys and a martini.

After returning to the table with the drinks, Sam asked, "So, what's the Center for Sex and Culture that you three went to earlier today?"

Karette answered, "The Center is located at 1349 Mission Street in The Mission, Sam, and I've worked there ever since I escaped from exotic dancing. Its mission 'is to provide judgment-free education, cultural events, a library/media archive, and other resources to audiences across the sexual and gender spectrum; and to research and disseminate factual information, framing and informing issues of public policy and public health.' It also 'aims to provide a community center for education, advocacy, research, and support to the widest range of people.'

"As an instance of what goes on there, the other day I joined a discussion group on the two ways that women are exploited in contemporary American society. The first way is 'overt exploitation', which deals with such activities as prostitution, pornography, adult entertainment and so on. Generally, these businesses are organized by men for the benefit of men. The second way is 'covert exploitation', and it may be more harmful to women in the long run because it's so pervasive. In this type of exploitation, women willingly agree to participate in activities that operate for the benefit of men and to the detriment of women in society.

"As an example, some San Francisco women occasionally put on what's known as 'lingerie parties', where the gals parade about scantily-clad. However, men also attend these events, though of course they're fully-clothed and their participation is merely to gawk at the ladies. So here's a situation where women willingly agree to be exploited at a blatantly sexist event, one that clearly goes against every tenet of feminism. It's sad to say that although throughout human history men's behavior has been the main problem for women, nowadays many women have become their own worst enemies."

"You're absolutely right, Karette," Yvette interjected. "Think back to our other discussion at the Center this afternoon on the differences between third-wave feminism and post-feminism. Third-wave feminism began in earnest during the early Nineties with Naomi Wolf's 1991 bestseller, *The Beauty Myth: How Images of Beauty Are Used Against Women*.

"In the first chapter, 'The Beauty Myth', she explains about the new war against women's liberation: 'Beauty is a currency system like the gold standard. Like any economy, it is determined by politics, and in the modern age in the West it is the last, best belief system that keeps male dominance intact. In assigning value to women in a vertical hierarchy according to a culturally imposed physical standard, it is an expression of power relations in which women must unnaturally compete for resources that men have appropriated for themselves.... There is no legitimate historical or biological justification for the beauty myth; what it is doing to women today is a result of nothing more than the need of today's power structure, economy, and culture to mount a counteroffensive against women.'

"Wolf's book deals with how the 'Beauty Myth' works through all aspects of a woman's life: Work, Culture, Religion, Sex, Hunger, and Violence. In the last chapter, 'Beyond the Beauty Myth', she offers an agenda for the future. And at the end of her book, Wolf writes about what part men can play in the emerging third wave of feminism: 'But helping women to take the myth apart is in men's own interests on an even deeper level: Their turn is next. Advertisers have recently figured out that undermining sexual self-confidence works whatever the targeted gender.... As this imagery focuses more closely on male sexuality, it will undermine the sexual self-esteem of men in general. Since men are more conditioned to be separate from their bodies, and to compete to inhuman excess, the male version could conceivably hurt men even more than the female version hurts women.'"

While the three ladies continued with their discussion, Sam thought about how very accurate Wolf's prediction was twenty years later. Everywhere he went and everything he heard told him that he wasn't manly enough for any woman. He was constantly bombarded by messages that his penis wasn't big enough, that it wasn't hard enough, that his erection didn't last long enough, and that his testosterone levels were far too low to ever give real pleasure to a woman. As well, he was continually told that his body was too hairy and that every part of it needed to be shaved or waxed, except for his scalp, which needed to have more hair grown or sewn onto it. Everything in life advised him that he was inadequate, but that there were expensive products available to alleviate his terribly flawed conditions. And though he never gave a name to it, he knew that he was forever inadequate due to "The Manly Myth" perpetrated everywhere in American society these days.

In addition, Sam thought about how he felt emotionally challenged by his friendship with Cosette, even though he felt closer to her now than when they were just "having sex" a year back. He'd never been friends with a woman before, and he'd never felt like sharing his ideas, feelings and anxieties about his life with any woman before. And yet, here he was closer to any woman he'd ever known, but without sleeping with her, without "making love" with her. He had no idea how this could be, for it was the first time that he'd ever experienced such an unusual relationship with a woman.

Sam considered whether it was even natural for a man to have such feelings for a woman he wasn't sleeping with. Everything in the media, in films, and in books told him that relationships should revolve solely around going to bed with somebody. It was never mentioned that a healthy relationship involved not just what went on in the bedroom, but maybe more importantly, what went on in the rest of the house - of shared interests, projects and dreams. He was beginning to understand that most men only experienced women as friends when they were also involved with them sexually. That was unfortunate, for most men were missing out on one of the more wonderful aspects of life.

While Sam thought more about his newly-emerging perception of women and himself, Yvette talked to Cosette and Karette about anti-feminism, "This reactionary movement denies at least one of the three principles of feminism: social relationships among men and women are neither natural nor divine, social arrangements among men and women favor men, and actions can be taken to transform these conditions into a more just civil agreement between the sexes.

"Susan Faludi dealt with these problems in her 1991 book, *Backlash: The Undeclared War Against American Women*: 'How can American women be in so much trouble at the same time that they are supposed to be so blessed?... The prevailing wisdom of the past decade has supported one, and only one, answer to this riddle: it must be all that equality that's causing all that pain. Women are unhappy precisely *because* they are free. Women are enslaved by their own liberation.... But what has made women unhappy in the last decade is not their "equality" - which they don't yet have - but the rising pressure to halt, and even reverse, women's quest for that equality.... Identifying feminism as women's enemy only furthers the ends of a backlash against women's equality, simultaneously deflecting attention from the backlash's central role and recruiting women to attack their own cause.'"

The Simple Art of Murder

The evening at an end, the four of them left the bar and caught a cab to Sam's place, dropping Karette at her apartment in The Mission along the way. Once at his building, Sam went in to first check if anyone was there, but found the place empty. He motioned for the other two to come in, and they went into the kitchen for some sandwiches and coffee. With their light meal out of the way, Cosette and Yvette covered themselves with a blanket on the Murphy, while Sam positioned a chair in the hallway to spend the night watching the front door with his gun in hand, this time loaded for possible action.

While the ladies slept, Sam searched his mind for an answer to the fundamental question: "Am I enough of a man to resolve the investigation?" And to answer that question, he thought about what Michael Kimmel wrote in the 2006 book, *Manhood in America: A Cultural History*: "Putting manhood in historical context presents it differently, as a constantly changing collection of meanings that we construct through our relationships with ourselves, with each other, and with our world. Manhood is neither static nor timeless. Manhood is not the manifestation of an inner essence; it's socially constructed. Manhood does not bubble up to consciousness from our biological constitution; it is created in our culture. In fact, the search for a transcendent, timeless definition of manhood is itself a sociological phenomenon - we tend to search for the timeless and eternal during moments of crisis, those points of transition when the old definitions no longer work and the new definitions are yet to be firmly established."

Sam also pondered on his personal sense of manhood, thinking back to Harvey C. Mansfield's 2006 work, *Manliness*: "Manliness. What is that?... Manliness seeks and welcomes drama and prefers times of war, conflict, and risk. Manliness brings change or restores order at moments when routine is not enough, when the plan fails, when the whole idea of rational control by modern science develops leaks. Manliness is the next-to-last resort, before resignation and prayer.... A manly man asserts himself so that he and the justice he demands are not overlooked. He rouses himself and seeks attention for what he deems important, sometimes something big..."

About an hour later, Cosette came out to the hallway and said, "Sam, I want to thank you for all your hard work on the investigation." She then caressed his face in her hands and kissed him lightly on the lips, the first time she'd done so since their split a year back.

Sam smiled at her as she returned to the Murphy and he thought: "Maybe she's the kind of dame I could wake up with in the morning. You can't say that about most broads." But he also knew that he should never let his guard down around her, not that any man should ever let his guard down around any woman, as Frank warned in *The Lady is a Tramp.*

His mind returning to what he now had to accomplish, for the next hour Sam organized his thoughts on how best to progress in the morning. First, he had to get Yvette out of the city and put Cosette into hiding. With his hands then free, he had to get to the office and plan the order of events that would have to proceed in a clock-work fashion. Sam knew that only in this way could he resolve "The Case of the Siren in the Sea." After having thought through his next day's actions, Sam then spent some time reading a 1950 Raymond Chandler article, *The Simple Art of Murder.*

Chinatown and Little Italy

A Proper Punishment in Chinatown

With the sun just starting to rise over an unaware and uncaring city, the three caught a cab to Cosette's apartment, where Yvette quickly packed her stuff. She said goodbye to Cosette and Sam, and next drove out of town for her own protection. Sam then said to Cosette, "I want you to go back in your apartment and not come out until I call you in the early evening after I've concluded my investigation."

Cosette unlocked the door of her apartment and then turned to Sam, "I'm worried, please don't let anything happen to you."

"Don't worry, Cosette, I know what I'm doing," Sam said trying to convince himself that he *did* know what he was doing.

As soon as Cosette locked her door, Sam caught a cab back to his apartment. Once there, he intended getting back to his usual schedule and daily rituals. However, instead of choosing a black tie, this morning he chose the red one, the tie that Cosette gave him a year before. As he put the tie on, his hand began to shake and he thought: "I can do this."

Sam's stomach was too churned up for breakfast at the Golden Coffee, so he walked straight to his office building along the shortest possible route. Once in his office, Sam felt completely disoriented and so spent the entire morning methodically planning what he had to do next. He first wrote an e-mail to his attorney, Sid Wise, detailing all he knew about the killings of Cosette's friend and the twin girls. He told Wise that in the event that something happened to him, he should forward the e-mail to the *Chronicle*. Sam also told him to keep a hard copy of the e-mail in his office safe, and he then printed off a copy for Tom.

At a quarter to two, Sam walked over to Market and turned west for the tramp up to Ellis. Once at Ellis, he made his way into John's Grill, where Tom waited for him at a table. John's Grill opened in

1908 and remains one of the best steak and seafood restaurants in the downtown area, despite what Herb Caen said about it many years ago. John's most famous patron was of course Sam's dad, Samuel Spade, and his presence is still felt in the image of the Maltese falcon on the front door canopy. His dad's presence is also felt on the menu. So as soon as he was seated, Sam and Tom ordered "Sam Spade's Lamb Chops, served with baked potato and sliced tomatoes," along with a couple of martinis.

Over lunch, Sam told his friend everything he knew about the case and gave him a copy of the e-mail to keep in a safe place. Sam then said, "I don't know what's going to happen to me, but if anything does, hand over the details of my investigation to anyone you trust at Central."

"Sam, I don't think there's anyone I can trust at Central anymore," Tom replied, "but I still have a few connections down at the Fed building. If anything happens to you, I'll make sure someone over at the Bureau is made aware of your investigation. And Sam, I don't want to know anything about what you're going to do next. Anyway, this is my last day on the job, so let's have another martini for the road."

"Good idea, Tom," Sam agreed, "and here's to the old times before this town got all screwy."

After Sam and Tom finished their chops and drinks, they said goodbye and Sam walked back down Market to his office. Once there, he first wrote a note to Gutt telling him that he called off his investigation into the killings. He also said that in the event that anything happened to either Cosette or himself, information detailing his investigation would be sent to the *Chronicle* and the Feds. He then lay down on the office couch and caught up on some much needed sleep.

Sam woke up around six in the evening and immediately went over to his office safe. He got out a new pair of gloves and a clean rod, which he loaded with bullets. He then left his office building, walked up Sutter to Kearny Street, and then turned north on Kearney to Bush Street. Sam next walked east on Bush to Sam's Grill at 374 Bush

Street and Belden Place, where he thought a martini would steady his nerves for what he had to do that evening. Sam's Grill opened at its present location in 1936, and today still serves some of the best seafood dishes in the city.

After downing his second martini, Sam looked at his watch and read seven o'clock, time to get the job done. He left Sam's Grill and walked west on Bush to Stockton Street, and then crossed over the top of the Stockton Tunnel. Continuing a few steps west, he stopped at the short dead-end alley at Burritt Street on the south side of Bush. Looking up on the building wall, he read a plaque.

> On approximately this spot,
> Miles Archer,
> partner of Sam Spade,
> was done in by
> Brigid O'Shaughnessy.

Though he knew his dad never liked Miles, he also knew that "when a man's partner is killed he's supposed to do something about it. It doesn't make any difference what you thought of him. He was your partner and you're supposed to do something about it."

Sam next walked back to Stockton, then north past The Ritz-Carlton. On the north side of the tunnel, he stopped at the top of the stairs to overlook Chinatown and to question what his destiny held in store for him. After a few unanswered moments, he took the stairs down to the northern entrance of the Stockton Tunnel. He then made his way along Stockton through Chinatown, not the tourist town on Grant Avenue, but the real Chinatown.

With twilight settling in upon the city, Sam continued along Stockton to Broadway, where he located the apartment building that Sammy told him about on the northwest corner of the intersection. And just as his friend said, the windows were boarded up on the third-floor corner room. Putting on his gloves, Sam picked the lock to open the building door and then made his way up to the third floor.

He first knocked on the apartment door, standing to one side as he did so. After hearing no answer, he picked the second lock.

Sam slowly opened the door and went inside, and then immediately checked that there was no one in the place. He once again looked at his watch, which read a quarter to eight. After he sat quietly in the apartment for another fifteen minutes, he heard steps at the door and a key being inserted into the lock. He quietly maneuvered himself behind the door and waited to capture a glimpse of a face. As the door opened, a man entered the apartment, with the light from the hallway illuminating his face. Sure enough, it was Sammy's dead ringer for Peter Lorre, the killer named Joe.

As the door began to close, Sam pulled his gun out and made ready to confront the man. After having watched *The Maltese Falcon* for what must have been an untold number of times, he knew he had to perform the scene exactly as he'd planned earlier in the day. When the door finally closed and the apartment light came on, Sam pistol-whipped Joe on the left side of his face and the killer fell to the ground. Sam's hands were shaking as he switched his gun to the other hand and pistol-whipped him again, this time on the right side. He was so furious that he could have pistol-whipped Joe for the rest of his life.

Lying semi-conscious on the floor and unable to move, Sam said to Joe, "You gave me no choice, Joe. There are many things a man shouldn't do in life. One of those is killing young girls. Now you'll see what it's like to die." Sam put one gloved hand over Joe's mouth and pinched the killer's nose with the other hand, drawing the life from him. After a few minutes, and with one last shaking of his arms and legs, Joe remained motionless. He was sleeping the big sleep.

Sam immediately put his gun away, turned out the light, and then made his way out of the apartment. Once out on the street, he took off his gloves and walked east on Broadway, disposing of his gun and gloves down one of the rain gutters along the way. He knew that when Gutt's goons found Joe, they'd dispose of the body in their own way and without bringing the cops into it. And he also knew that even if the cops did find out about the killing, there wouldn't be an investigation, otherwise there'd be too much scrutiny by the press. Nobody at Central or City Hall wanted that, especially as it happened in Chinatown. It was just another lowlife homicide in the city, another statistic that would go unreported in the morning paper.

While walking east on Broadway toward Columbus, Sam phoned Cosette and told her, "Honey, it's safe to leave your apartment now. Our investigation is finally over. It's time to celebrate, so get ready for a night on the town. And give Yvette a call and tell her that the investigation has been wrapped up." After looking at his watch, he continued, "It's half past eight now, so meet me at Bocce in an hour." After ending his call, Sam decided to never tell Cosette about what he'd done that night.

Sam continued down Broadway to the club where the two dead girls were once kept and barged straight in the front door without paying the mandatory cover charge. He was immediately surrounded by a couple of bouncers, one of them being William, who Sam addressed, "Looks like those bruises are healing nicely, William." Sam laughed at him and then walked over to where a fat man was sitting at a register counting his money.

"You must be Gutt, and you do look a lot like Sydney Greenstreet," Sam said as he reached into his coat pocket and pulled out the note he wrote that afternoon. "I think you'll want to read this."

The fat man unfolded and looked over the note. Sam then told him, "I also think you'll want to send a couple of your goons over to that apartment at Stockton and Broadway."

His business done, Sam turned around and left the club. And as he walked away he thought about something that Raymond Chandler wrote in the 1950 essay, *The Simple Art of Murder*: "Down these mean streets a man must go who is not himself mean, who is neither tarnished nor afraid.... He has a range of awareness that startles you, but it belongs to him by right, because it belongs to the world he lives in.... If there were enough like him, I think the world would be a very safe place to live in, and yet not too dull to be worth living in."

A Lovely Lady in Little Italy

Sam walked back up Broadway to Columbus, then north to Grant Avenue. Relieved that the case was finally over, he breathed easier as he sauntered up Grant through Little Italy to Green Street and the Bocce Cafe at 478 Green Street. Bocce, with its woodsy interior and garden dining, offers excellent Italian dishes served with light jazz on Friday and Saturday nights. It was only nine o'clock, so he sat at the bar and enjoyed his usual martini while waiting for Cosette to arrive.

At precisely half past nine, Cosette walked in all dolled up in a loose-fitting black and white polka dot blouse, with a lovely red tie at the neck lying just off to the side. She was a knockout, and every head in the place turned to look at her, which of course she enjoyed immensely. They were shown to a table near the jazz trio and ordered two bottles of wine, Chardonnay for her and Chianti for him. They also ordered the "Antipasto Della Casa (for 2): A sampling of authentic Italian antipasti, including mozzarella, caprese, smoked salmon, bruschetta, olives, roasted bell peppers, grilled vegetables, marinated baby artichokes, prosciutto and salami."

While enjoying the wine and antipasto, Cosette said, "Sam, thanks for wearing the red tie I gave you a year ago. I didn't think I'd ever see you in any tie but a black one. Now, tell me the truth, is the investigation really over?"

"Yes, Cosette, and we won't have any trouble with those Broadway goons anymore," Sam answered. "However, you can no longer try to directly rescue the young girls in the clubs. It's far too risky and far too dangerous. You'll have to find another way to help them."

"I already thought about that, Sam," Cosette replied. "I'm going to volunteer my time to BAYSWAN to force the city to address health, safety and exploitation issues in the adult entertainment industry. Maybe that'll make the city a safer place for young girls and women."

"I hope so, Cosette, I hope so," Sam responded.

Sam then thought: "If she only knew how connected the sex industry was to the city's far-reaching power structure. In any large town the politicians and all the moneyed interests needed a thriving flesh trade. The fact of the matter was, without a multitude of prostitutes and sex clubs, no conference or convention would ever be held in oh-so-liberal San Francisco, a town where anything goes. Like every other place in the world, the City by the Bay was run by powerful men who weren't particularly concerned about the welfare of women. But though no one ever touched the big guys, Sam knew that at least a few of the little ones dropped every now and then."

After finishing the antipasto, for their main dinner they shared the "Cioppino: crab, prawns, salmon, calamari, clams and mussels, served in a bowl with pasta on the side." They were both too full for dessert after the meal, and so just finished the wine and listened to the jazz trio. Before leaving, Sam walked up to the group and requested a song, *Polka Dots and Moonbeams*. And as the trio played, Cosette and Sam danced slowly as he whispered the lyrics in her ear. At the end of the song, the two kissed passionately on the lips. He knew immediately that he was once again under Cosette's spell, and that he could no longer deny to himself his overwhelming desire for her. He desperately needed to be with her, to be her lover, to be everything to her, and she everything to him.

With dinner over, Cosette and Sam left Bocce to have a nightcap at Specs'. They held hands as they walked along Grant to Columbus, with the light of a full moon hitting her in such a way at one point that he thought: "Ella was so right that *Moonlight Becomes You*." Continuing on, they crossed Broadway and walked down the street to the speakeasy. Once inside the bar, they sat down at Sam's usual table underneath the Bogey photo before he ordered drinks, a whiskey for her and a martini for himself, also as usual.

After returning to the table with the drinks, Cosette said, "Sam, do you remember that I told you in Vesuvio a few days ago that I always had a problem with your work as a private investigator, that I was petrified by the violence in your life and the gun that you always carried on you. Well, I now understand that I must learn to accommodate your ways, because that's how you define yourself, as a PI."

"Cosette, I actually think I've defined myself too much as a PI," Sam admitted, "and I don't want to live that way anymore. I can honestly tell you that this case has changed me and I'm hanging up the guns for good. I still feel satisfaction in what I do and I know I'm good at it, but I don't want to be *this* sort of private investigator ever again. It's not healthy for me, and anyway, I've got a case starting Monday that I think will perhaps help send me off in a new direction. What about you?"

"Just like you, Sam," Cosette answered, "I'm going to make some changes in my life too. It's time for me to move on from 'The Siren in the Sea' and other provocative performances. My creative talents need to flourish in other directions."

"I'm very glad to hear that, Cosette," Sam said, "and hopefully I can be helpful to you in the process. And if you don't mind, perhaps we could pick up where we left off a year ago. I know I'm now ready to finally spend the entire night with you?" And while waiting for her response to his suggestion, Sam listened to Cricket as he played the melody *How Little We Know*, while Slim sang the lyrics.

Just then, Cosette's phone went off and she spoke into it, "No problem, I'll be down there in ten minutes." After putting her phone away, she told Sam, "They need me in the aquarium at The Club for a midnight performance. I'll call you in the morning." After draining her whiskey, she kissed Sam on the cheek, got up, and put her coat on. And as she walked towards the door, Cricket played a jazzed-up version of *How Little We Know*, with Cosette shaking her hips to the music while every male in the place longingly watched her exit the bar.

With Cosette now gone, Sam went to the bar for one last martini. After returning to his table, he realized that she wouldn't call him in the morning, nor would she call him during the rest of Sunday. He'd served her purposes for the time being, and he wouldn't hear from her until his services were needed again. He knew as well that she would always say she was giving up "The Siren in the Sea," but she would never actually give it up, for Cosette needed the attention of the crowd to confirm *her* very existence.

As Sam finished his drink, it dawned on him that the illusion perpetuated by the "The Siren in the Sea" was nothing more than the illusion that the City of San Francisco perpetuated about itself in order to attract the attention of the world and to confirm *its* very existence. The ingratiating image of a city "where little cable cars climb halfway to the stars" was one far removed from the reality of the real San Francisco. For like his dad always reminded him: "Most things in San Francisco can be bought, or taken." He then asked himself: "Is this all there is? Is there nothing more?"

Little did Sam know that the answers to his eternal questions would begin to be resolved the day after next, when he'd meet a man that would send him on a journey to parts unknown. After finishing his drink, Sam walked out of Specs' into a cold and damp San Francisco night, and then strolled south along Columbus towards his apartment. As he quickly disappeared into the lingering summer fog, Sam heard a melody whispered in his ears by a crooner named Tony, one titled... *I Left My Heart in San Francisco.*

The Philosophical Investigator

On Sunday Sam remained near his phone, which stayed silent throughout the day, just as he'd predicted the night before. On Monday morning he was back at his usual schedule and daily rituals, when he heard a knock on the office door. He got up to let in his newest client, a distinguished-looking older gentleman, impeccably dressed in a suit and tie from an age when men were far more meticulous about their appearance. He sat down in the client's chair and Sam asked, "May I call you Will."

"Will is alright by me," he responded, "and should I call you Sam?"

"That's fine," Sam replied. "Would you care for a cup of coffee?"

Will did, so Sam poured them both a cup and then questioned his client about the case, "I understand from our short telephone conversation of last week that you have what you consider a rather unique case for me. But before I agree to take on the investigation, could you please explain a little about yourself?"

"Before retiring," Will began, "I was a writer of books on philosophy and history. In a sense, you might say I was in the same line of work as you. Though rather than being a private investigator, I was what's called a philosophical investigator, or as the French say, *le flâneur philosophique*."

"Excuse me, Will," Sam interrupted. "Before going on you should know that I'm not familiar with much about philosophy or history. And I have no idea what *le flâneur philosophique* might be."

"I don't believe that will be a problem, Sam," Will continued, "for I have an agency in mind that will help you as regards the necessary particulars of those two trains of thought, at least as they pertain to the case. However, what I do need to know is do you have a problem with traveling overseas, for that agency is in Paris?"

Sam thought for a moment and then said, "No, I suppose I don't mind as long as the money's good."

"Now as to the money," Will replied, "I'm afraid I can only cover your expenses. Is that going to be a problem?"

Sam thought for a moment and then realized that he'd become somewhat curious about where this case was heading. So as he'd no other cases going on, nor any new ones in the foreseeable future, he answered, "No, covering my expenses is fine. But before giving you a final answer about taking on your case, can you tell me some of the particulars?"

Will reflected on Sam's question for a moment, apparently lost in thought, and then slowly said, "This may sound slightly odd to you, but something has gone missing."

"That's fine, Will," Sam interjected, "I've been on cases involving missing persons or stolen monies or valuable objects plenty of times."

"Yes, Sam," Will continued, "you no doubt have been on such cases, but I doubt ever on an investigation such as this. What has gone missing is not a person or money or a valuable object, though it is indeed valuable, and perhaps the most valuable thing in the world. What has gone missing is 'Modernity'."

Needless to say, Sam looked at him with questioning eyes and said, "What are you talking about? I've never even heard of Modernity? I can't see how I would be of any value to you on this case."

Will first smiled and then responded, "Please don't rush to any hasty decisions involving this investigation, for you're not the only person that has never heard about Modernity. In fact, most people living today haven't heard about it, which is probably why it has gone missing. The period we historians call Modernity began roughly 500 years ago, though sometime during the last century it reportedly began to disappear, first in Europe and then in America. If you decide to take on this case, your task will be to search for this most valuable object. However, if you are unable to find it, then you will attempt to discover what has replaced it, which I will tentatively call 'Postmodernity', leaving that term undefined for the time being."

"Go on, Will," Sam said, with his curiosity in this new case now quite overwhelming.

"I can see that this case does indeed interest you," Will said. "Fortunately, you don't have to work on it alone in Paris. I've contacted the Paris branch of the 'Pascal, Descartes, Voltaire and Rousseau Philosophical Investigation Services' to help you in your search, and they sent me a packet of instructions to give to you."

Will handed him the packet and then continued, "I have also arranged tickets for your flight and modest accommodations in an area of Paris known as Montmartre. Do you have any questions, Sam?"

"Yes," Sam answered, "plenty of them, though I have the feeling they won't begin to be addressed until I get to Paris."

"Very good," Will responded, "and here's an ATM card to handle your daily expenses while in the City of Light. By the way, while working on this case please take time to enjoy the sights and the sounds, and the foods and the wines, of the most culturally-preoccupied city in the world. And as well, don't forget to fall in love while in Paris, not only with the city, but also with the uniquely beautiful women that call her home. For Paris is there to be loved through the mind, the body and the heart." With that, Will stood up, shook Sam's hand, and left the office, saying as he went, "I'll talk to you when you get back."

The first thing Sam did after Will left was to check the departure date on the ticket printout, which indicated that he was leaving San Francisco in the late afternoon for a stay in Paris of two weeks. So he closed up the office, had some lunch, and went to his apartment to pack a few things for the flight. Once done, and after looking forever for his passport, Sam walked down to BART and caught the train out to SFO.

Sam's flight to Paris took off on time, and after a few hours and a few martinis he fell into a deep sleep. However, somewhere in time and place he experienced the beginning of a profound change, when the private investigator Sam Marlowe disappeared from the world and was replaced by the philosophical investigator Sam Marlowe.

Needless to say, only Jacques Barzun in his 2000 masterpiece, *From Dawn to Decadence*, could explain the reason for this unique transformation: "Is this a mystery or not? No answer seems conclusive if we ponder any important changes in ourselves... occasionally [caused] by an emotional shock. Again, when our minds undergo sudden, profound alterations - in opinion or belief, in love, or in what is called artistic inspiration - what is the ultimate cause? We see the results, but grasp the chain of reasoning at a link well below the hook from which it hangs."

So began my newest investigation, one I named "The Case of the Missing Modernity."

The Private Investigator Walking Tours

San Francisco is a great city for walking tours, especially when they pass by any of the spots mentioned in *The Private Investigator*. So to aid the urban walker in that endeavor, below are a few tours that pass by all the prominent sites in the book. And for those new to the city and hoping to avoid getting lost, take along any of the tourist maps available around town.

Fisherman's Wharf to North Beach

This walking tour begins at the Buena Vista Cafe in Fisherman's Wharf. It then heads up Columbus to pass by Piazza Pellegrini, Washington Square, Caffé Roma, Original Joe's, and Bocce Cafe in North Beach. The tour continues through North Beach to Broadway, The Beat Museum and City Lights, to end at Vesuvio, Tosca Cafe, and Specs'.

> Begin the tour at the Buena Vista Cafe at 2765 Hyde Street, which sits across from the Powell-Hyde Cable Car Turnaround. (Enjoy an Irish coffee in the café where Sam thought back to his investigation, "The Case of the Wit and Wisdom of Herb Caen.")

> Walk east on Beach Street to Columbus Avenue, then southeast on Columbus along the western side of the street.

> Continue walking up Columbus to Piazza Pellegrini at 659 Columbus Avenue, which sits across from Washington Square. (Enjoy a slice of pie and a glass of vino in the restaurant where Sam thought back to his investigation, "The Case of the Man Who Loved Pizza.")

Continue walking up Columbus to Union Street, then cross over to Washington Square. (In the center of the square near some trees is the Benjamin Franklin statue, where Cosette's friend was killed trying to rescue the two twin girls.)

If time permits, cross Union and walk up Columbus to Caffé Roma at 526 Columbus Avenue. (Enjoy an espresso and a cannoli, as did Cosette and Yvette before meeting with Karette in North Beach.)

Walk to the northeast end of the Square and then cross over Union to Original Joe's at 601 Union Street. (Enjoy a fine Italian meal in the restaurant where Sam thought back to his investigation, "The Case of the Troubled Techies.")

Walk south on Stockton Street to Green Street, then east on Green and across Grant Avenue to Bocce Cafe at 478 Green Street. (Enjoy a fine Italian meal and Friday/Saturday night jazz in the restaurant where Cosette and Sam celebrated solving "The Case of the Siren in the Sea.")

Walk south on Grant to Columbus, then southeast along Columbus to Broadway.

Walk east on the northern side of Broadway to the Beat Museum at 540 Broadway. (Enjoy exploring the history of the San Francisco Beats.)

Walk back along Broadway to Columbus and then cross to the western side of the avenue.

Walk south along Columbus to City Lights at 261 Columbus Avenue. (Enjoy exploring the bookstore and head downstairs to where Cosette, Yvonne and Karette discussed what was going on in the Broadway clubs.)

Walk south along Columbus to Jack Kerouac Alley and then cross over to Vesuvio at 255 Columbus Avenue. (Enjoy a pleasant libation in a bar dedicated to the Beat writer Jack Kerouac and where Cosette told Yvette about Sam's investigation, "The Case of the Unintentional Earthquake.")

Walk north on Columbus to Broadway, then cross to the eastern side of Columbus.

Walk south on Columbus to Tosca Cafe at 242 Columbus Avenue. (Enjoy a fine Italian meal and a bottle of vino in a famed San Francisco restaurant and bar.)

Walk next door to Specs' Twelve Adler Museum Cafe at 12 William Saroyan Place. (Enjoy another pleasant libation in a bar where Sam thought back to his investigation, "The Case of the Gyrating Gender.")

Lower Knob to The Financial District

This walking tour begins outside Sam's apartment and first heads to his usual breakfast place, the Golden Coffee Shop. It then follows his usual morning footsteps past the Geary Theatre, Lefty O'Doul's, Union Square, Marquard's Smoke Shop, Herbert's Grill, and John's Grill. The tour then heads down Market to end in the lobby of Sam's office building at One Eleven Sutter.

Begin the tour at the 891 Post Street apartment building of Dashiell Hammett, Sam Spade, and his son, Sam Marlowe. (Sam's apartment can be seen from street level when looking up from the southeast corner of Post and Hyde Street, and read the plaque on the wall outside the entrance to the building.)

Walk east on Post to Leavenworth Street, then north on Leavenworth to Sutter Street.

On the southwest corner of the intersection is the Golden Coffee Shop at 901 Sutter Street. (Enjoy a hearty breakfast in a coffee shop that's definitely old school.)

Walk south on Leavenworth to Geary Street, then east on the southern side of Geary to Jones Street.

As a detour, walk south on Jones to the Bourbon & Branch at 501 Jones Street in The Tenderloin. (Enjoy a shot of bourbon - or two or three - in the speakeasy where Sam thought back to his investigation, "The Case of the Extraordinary Emperor.")

Return to Geary and then walk east to the Geary Theatre at 415 Geary Street. (If open, enter the lobby and look around to see where Sam Spade met with Joel Cairo.)

Walk east on Geary to Lefty O'Doul's Restaurant and Cocktail Lounge at 333 Geary Street. (Enjoy a pleasant libation in the sports bar where Sam thought back to his investigation, "The Case of the Snobby Sleuth.")

Walk east on Geary to Powell Street and Union Square. (Enjoy the scene in the Square.)

Walk south on the western side of Powell to O'Farrell Street. (On the southwest corner of the intersection is the old sign for Marquard's Smoke Shop at 167 Powell Street, the place where Sam Spade picked up his smokes.)

Walk south on Powell a few doors to the former location of Herbert's Grill at 161 Powell Street. (This was once the place where Sam Spade often ate a meal.)

Walk south on Powell to Ellis Street and cross over to the southern side of Ellis.

Walk east on Ellis to John's Grill at 63 Ellis Street. (Observe the image of the Maltese falcon above the entrance, placed there to commemorate where Sam Spade often ate a meal. Enter the restaurant to enjoy a pleasant libation and a great meal while looking at all the photographs of the famous patrons that ever did the same.)

Walk east on Ellis to Market Street, then along Market to Montgomery Street. (Enjoy the hustle and bustle along Market in the location where Sam thought back to his investigation, "The Case of the Pervasive Parades.")

Walk north along the western side of Montgomery to Sutter Street and the 22-story One Eleven Sutter building at 111 Sutter Street, the former Financial District location of The Hunter Dulin Building. (Enter the building to observe a photo of a scene from *The Maltese Falcon* in the lobby's picture gallery.)

The Financial District to The Embarcadero

This walking tour begins at Sam's office and first heads to Tadich Grill. It then continues down to the Ferry Building and follows The Embarcadero past Sinbad's, the Hi Dive, Red's Java House, and the Java House, to end at the Giants' ballpark.

Begin the tour at Sam's office building at 111 Sutter Street.

Walk north on Montgomery to California Street, then east on California to Tadich Grill at 240 California Street. (Enjoy a pleasant libation and a great seafood meal in the grill where

Sam thought back to his investigation, "The Case of Mark Twain in San Francisco.")

Walk east on California to Drumm Street and then north on Drumm to Washington Street.

Walk east on Washington to The Embarcadero and then cross to the eastern side of the street at Pier 1.

Walk north on The Embarcadero to Pier 3. (The northern side of the pier is the probable location of where the *La Paloma* was accidently set on fire by Casper Gutman, Joel Cairo and Wilmer Cook, and also where Brigid O'Shaughnessy and Captain Jacobi had dinner while deciding what to do with the Maltese falcon.)

Walk south on The Embarcadero to the Ferry Building. (Enjoy pleasant libations and plenty of eats at any of the shops inside or outside the building.)

Exit the back of the Ferry Building and walk south to Sinbad's Pier 2 Restaurant. (Enjoy a fine martini and a great view of the San Francisco - Oakland Bay Bridge in the restaurant where Sam thought back to his investigation, "The Case of the World Series Earthquake.")

Walk south along The Embarcadero to the Hi Dive at Pier 28. (Enjoy another fine martini in a bar where Sam pistol-whipped his tail in the outdoor seating area.)

Walk south along The Embarcadero to Red's Java House at Pier 30. (Enjoy a great meal at the outdoor tables that overlook the bay and the bridge.)

Walk south along The Embarcadero to the Java House at Pier 40. (Enjoy the Game Day Special, a dog and a beer or a burger and a beer, at the outdoor tables that look out over South Beach Harbor.)

Walk south along The Embarcadero to the Giants' ballpark. (Enjoy a day watching the city's favorite team play America's favorite pastime, but first walk to the south end of the stadium and pay homage to the greatest all-around ballplayer ever, Willie Mays.)

The Haight to The Fillmore

This walking tour begins at Golden Gate Park in the Upper Haight and then heads to the Lower Haight, to end in The Fillmore at the Sheba Piano Lounge.

Begin the tour in the Upper Haight at the west end of Haight Street across from Golden Gate Park. (Golden Gate Park is where Sam investigated "The Case of the Summer of Rousseau" during the fourth "Summer of Love" festival.)

Walk east on Haight to Ashbury Street. (This notorious intersection is where Sam began his investigation, "The Case of the Summer of Rousseau.")

Walk east on Haight past Buena Vista Park to Fillmore Street in the Lower Haight.

Walk north on Fillmore to Ellis Street and The Fillmore. (This street is the southern end of the annual Fillmore Street Jazz Festival, which extends north to Jackson Street.)

Walk on the western side of Fillmore to the Sheba Piano Lounge at 1419 Fillmore Street. (Enjoy a pleasant libation, a great meal and some fine jazz at the piano bar where the pianist Sammy gave Sam the necessary information to solve "The Case of the Siren in the Sea.")

The Mission to The Castro

This walking tour begins in The Mission and then heads to The Castro, to end at Twin Peaks Tavern.

Begin the tour in The Mission on Valencia Street near 19th Street.

Walk south on Valencia to 19th Street.

Walk west on 19th to Delores Street.

Walk west through Delores Park to 19th Street in The Castro.

Walk west on 19th to Castro Street.

Walk north on Castro to Twin Peaks Tavern at 401 Castro Street near Market Street. (Enjoy a pleasant libation in the bar where Cosette, Yvette, Karette and Sam relaxed on the night before wrapping up the investigation, "The Case of the Siren in the Sea.")

The Financial District to Chinatown

This walking tour begins at Sam's office and first heads to Sam's Grill. It then continues past where Sam Spade's partner was killed, to end in Chinatown.

Begin the tour at Sam's office building at 111 Sutter Street.

Walk west on Sutter to Kearny Street.

Walk north on Kearney to Bush Street.

Walk east on Bush to Sam's Grill at 374 Bush Street and Belden Place. (Enjoy a pleasant libation and a great meal at the restaurant where Sam organized his thoughts on how to end his investigation, "The Case of the Siren in the Sea.")

Walk west on Bush to Stockton Street.

Walk across to the western side of the Stockton Tunnel.

Walk a few steps west on the southern side of Bush to the short dead-end alley at Burritt Street. (Observe the plaque on the wall that indicates where Miles Archer, Sam Spade's partner, was killed by Brigid O'Shaughnessy.)

Walk a few steps east on Bush to Stockton.

Walk north on Stockton over the Stockton Tunnel to Sacramento Street. (This is the spot above the tunnel where Sam looked out over Chinatown and thought about what he had to do next to end his investigation, "The Case of the Siren in the Sea.")

Return to street-level and then walk on Stockton to Broadway. (On the northwest corner of the intersection is the apartment building where on the third floor, Sam pistol-whipped and suffocated the killer of Cosette's friend and the two twin girls.)

Walk north on Broadway to Columbus. (Enjoy a pleasant libation at either Vesuvio or Specs' or preferably both.)

Land's End to Golden Gate Bridge

This walking tour begins at the Cliff House at Land's End and follows the southern edge of San Francisco Bay, to end at the Golden Gate Bridge.

Begin the tour in the The Bistro at the Cliff House at 1090 Point Lobos Avenue. (Enjoy a pleasant libation and a fine meal while overlooking the Pacific Ocean and Seal Rocks in a restaurant where Cosette and Sam worked on "The Case of the Siren in the Sea.")

Walk east on Point Lobos Avenue to the path heading down to the Sutro Baths.

Walk down the dirt path to the southern end of Point Lobos and the ruins of the Sutro Baths. (This is where Cosette identified the body of the first dead girl while Sam distracted the cops.)

Walk back up the path from Sutro Baths to Point Lobos Avenue.

Walk east on Point Lobos past the parking lot to Merrie Way.

Walk north on Merrie Way to the start of the Coastal Trail.

Walk east on the Coastal Trail which follows the coastline along the Golden Gate National Recreation Area to El Camino del Mar. (Enjoy the serenity of Land's End, Lincoln Park,

Deadman's Point, Eagle's Point, and the Marin Headlands on the northern side of the entrance to the bay.)

Walk east on El Camino del Mar to Sea Cliff Avenue.

Walk north on Sea Cliff to the entrance to China Beach Park.

Walk down to China Beach. (Enjoy a spectacular view of the Golden Gate Bridge.)

Walk up to Sea Cliff.

Walk east on Sea Cliff to 25th Avenue.

Walk north and then turn east on 25th to the Coastal Trail.

Walk east on the Coastal Trail to Baker Beach. (Enjoy another spectacular view of the Golden Gate Bridge.)

Walk east and then southeast on the Coastal Trail to Lincoln Boulevard.

Walk on Lincoln to the Battery to Bluffs Trail.

Walk west and then north on the Battery to Bluffs Trail to the Coastal Trail at the Golden Gate Bridge.

Walk east and then south on the Coastal Trail to the Golden Gate Bridge Lookout. (If time permits, enjoy a walk on the bridge.)

Golden Gate Bridge to Fisherman's Wharf

This walking tour begins at the Golden Gate Bridge and first follows the southern edge of San Francisco Bay to Crissy Field. It then continues along the bay to The Marina and Aquatic Park, to end at Fisherman's Wharf.

Walk north on the Coastal Trail to the Battery East Trail.

Walk east on the Battery East Trail, then take any of the dirt paths down to Long Avenue. (If time permits, enjoy a walk west on Long to Marine Drive, then west on Marine to Fort Point.)

Walk on the San Francisco Bay Trail past Torpedo Wharf to Marine Drive. (This is where Sam identified the body of the second dead girl.)

Walk east on Marine to the San Francisco Bay Trail. (Enjoy a tour of the Gulf of the Farallones National Marine Sanctuary.)

Walk east on the San Francisco Bay Trail to the Golden Gate Promenade.

Walk east on the Golden Gate Promenade along Crissy Field. (Enjoy a spectacular view of the Golden Gate Bridge, the Crissy Field Marsh, and Alcatraz.)

Walk east on the Golden Gate Promenade to E Beach. (The bathroom at E Beach is where Sam pistol-whipped his tail for a second time.)

Walk east, southeast and then south on the Golden Gate Promenade to the San Francisco Bay Trail.

Walk east and then north on the San Francisco Bay Trail. (Enjoy the boats at the Yacht Harbor.)

Walk east on the San Francisco Bay Trail. (Enjoy the action on Marina Green.)

Walk south and then east on the San Francisco Bay Trail. (Enjoy the boats at Gashouse Cove.)

Walk south on the San Francisco Bay Trail to Marina Boulevard.

Walk east on the path from Marina to Fort Mason Great Meadow.

Walk east on the path to Van Ness Avenue.

Walk out to the end of Aquatic Park Pier. (Enjoy another spectacular view of the Golden Gate Bridge and Alcatraz.)

Walk south on Van Ness to the Aquatic Park path.

Walk around the Aquatic Park path to Jefferson Street.

Walk east on Jefferson to the Gold Dust Lounge at 165 Jefferson Street. (Enjoy a pleasant libation in the bar's new location.)

The Private Investigator Songbook

Although San Francisco is a great city to walk in, an urban explorer also needs a pleasant song to enjoy along the way. Fortunately, *The Private Investigator* offers a wide selection of tunes to choose from, and they're all classics. With that in mind, please get in touch with the author and he'll send you a list of the particulars for all the tunes in the book: a YouTube site for listening to the song, the composer(s), a source the song appeared in, the instrumentalist(s), and the singer(s). Using the list, the traveler can easily copy and paste the YouTube address for each song into whatever tech device your social existence is now dependent upon.

The Private Invesigator Purpose

The reasons for writing this book are threefold. The first reason is to offer the residents of and the visitors to San Francisco a glimpse of the more interesting features concerning the city, both past and present. The second is to present the general reader a detective story involving the exploitation of girls and women in the adult entertainment industry. The third reason is to use the materials in the book with secondary students as one way of introducing learners to the history and tenets of feminism and the women's rights movement.

All royalties from the sales of this book go to support the Data Analysis Project, an educational concern coordinated by Ken Ewell. The first goal of the project is to work with public school teachers to increase their quantitative and statistical literacy skills, and to develop curriculum to improve the classroom learning experiences of their students in mathematics. The second goal is to prepare educators and learners for the *Common Core State Standards for Mathematics* program and the online *Smarter Balanced* testing system. The third goal is to organize a parent and guardian support group to address concerns and questions brought on by the *CCSSM* program and the *SB* system. The fourth goal of the project is to establish a two-year team- and technology-based workplace in exploratory and confirmatory data analysis as an alternative to the traditional one-year *Advanced Placement Statistics* course.

Ken can be contacted at *kenewell.noworriesmate@yahoo.com* or at the The Investigator Trilogy page on Facebook.